Unexpected Mr. Right

By
Kelley Nyrae

Other books by Kelley Nyrae
Getting Lucky with Luciano
The Emperor anthology – Trenton's Terms

Noire Passion is an imprint of Parker Publishing LLC.

Copyright © 2008 by Kelley Vitollo
Published by Parker Publishing LLC
12523 Limonite Avenue, Suite #440-438
Mira Loma, California 91752
www.parker-publishing.com

All rights reserved. This book is protected under the copyright laws of the United States of America. No part of this publication may be reproduced, stored in a retrieval system, or transmitted in any form or by any means—electronic, mechanical, photocopying, recording, or otherwise—without the prior written permission of the publisher.

This book is a work of fiction. Characters, names, locations, events and incidents (in either a contemporary and/or historical setting) are products of the author's imagination and are being used in an imaginative manner as a part of this work of fiction. Any resemblance to actual events, locations, settings, or persons, living or dead, is entirely coincidental.

ISBN: 978-1-60043-049-7
First Edition

Manufactured in the United States of America
Printed by Bang Printing, Brainard MN
Distributed by BookMasters, Inc. 1-800-537-6727
Cover Design by JaxadoraDesigns.com

Dedication

This book is dedicated to my best fried, my husband, Dominic. You support me beyond belief, love me through my worst as well as my best and have given me two beautiful girls who mean the world to me. I look forward to growing old with you by my side.

Acknowledgment

Thank you to the Landis Shores Oceanfront Inn in Half Moon Bay California for letting me set Nico and Tabby's weekend getaway in your beautiful bed and breakfast. Another big thanks to one of my very best friends, Tonya for being my second set of eyes and also to Travis for his help with a cooking recipe. Last but not least thank you to Jackie and Miriam for all that you have given me. I'll never forget it.

Unexpected Mr. Right

By
Kelley Nyrae

Chapter One

Tabitha Harris sat in her San Francisco office looking over paperwork for a new client. The woman had eccentric ideas for what she wanted for the new interior of her home. Bright colors and loud modern designs, nothing at all like her own taste but she had no doubt that she'd pull it off. It would be a struggle, creating a design the woman would like and not making herself vomit in the process, but she'd do it. Madeline Jones provided her the perfect distraction at just the right time.

Leaning back in her beige office chair, Tabby picked up the invitation to her best friend Kaylee's wedding. She had the whole thing memorized word for word, she'd picked what it said, chose the design for the card, volunteered to do the decorating. Their other best friend Brianna was supposed to be helping but Bri wasn't into the whole wedding thing like she was. When she really needed her, Bri would step in. Otherwise Tabby ran the show on this one.

The entire wedding madness made her heart ache.

Get over it, girl. She threw the pale yellow invitation on her desk. *Kaylee is your best friend. Push your jealousy aside and just be happy for her*. Not that she wasn't happy for her. She was, she just hurt too and sometimes that emotion overpowered the other.

A few months before, Kaylee, who never planned to marry or fall in love ended up with the man of her dreams. For months Kaylee, Brianna and herself spent their Friday nights at Luciano's, an Italian restaurant, for girl's night out. Since the first time they walked into the restaurant Kaylee had it bad for Luciano. Finally, after going at things in a round about way they ended up together.

Luciano was a great guy. They were perfect for each other. But she couldn't help but wonder what she did wrong. Why someone who didn't want love, who didn't want that happily ever after like Kaylee hadn't found it so quickly without any of the heartbreak. She wanted to have her dreams come true. She wanted to be marrying her Mr. Right along with her best friend.

Hell, they didn't even have to be getting married but she wanted to at least find the right guy, know what it felt like to be in love and to have someone else love you completely in return. Her parents had had that. All she'd ever wanted was to be as important to someone as her parents were to each other. They were *all* that mattered in each others eyes. Nothing else, just each other. Not even her.

Someday, she told herself. One day she'd have an intense emotional and physical connection with a man. One that felt the same way about her and only her. Not like the losers she'd run upon in the past.

A picture of Nico, Luciano's cousin popped into her head. They'd shared a hot kiss a few months ago and since then she thought about him at the weirdest times. The guy was a ladies man if she ever saw one. He had a different date for every night of the week and damn he could flirt. Since meeting him he'd set his flirtatious sights on her. She knew he wasn't serious but that didn't mean he didn't affect her. All he had to do is look at her with those sultry, brown eyes and she wanted to melt into a puddle on the floor.

She knew he wasn't the forever type of man, but that didn't stop Tabby from wanting him. He attracted her like no man had in a long while. Maybe ever. He was the embodiment of everything she knew she had to avoid. Bri and Kay always told her she went after the wrong men. If he was a heartbreaker, she somehow always found him and handed her heart over on a silver platter. Nico was definitely a heartbreaker. Gorgeous. But a heartbreaker all the same.

Tabby tossed her long, dark hair over her shoulder and glanced at her clock. It read 6:45 which meant she had fifteen minutes to get to Luciano's to meet Bri and Kaylee. What had always been carefree night just about the girls now included seeing her best friend deliriously happy with her fiancé and trying to pretend Nico's advances didn't faze her. *Yeah right*. The man made her sizzle with desire.

Nico was all about sex, desire, and giving into those desires for a quick roll between the sheets would be a disaster. She knew it, he knew it, everyone knew it. If she could roll like that he'd be the one she'd do it with, hell, if she gave him the chance he might even be able to convert her which is exactly why she didn't give him the time of day.

Tabby grabbed her suit jacket off the back of her chair and snatched her black, Gucci purse off her desk, before heading for the door. Tonight they'd be talking about wedding plans for Kaylee and Luciano. Their big day was only a couple months away and they still had to make final plans for the last of the decorations. She had a few more ideas she wanted to tell Kaylee about. Since weddings and decorating both fell into the "Tabby's kind of thing" category she'd done most of the work. Not that she minded in the least.

Stepping outside into the cool, San Francisco evening air, Tabby held up her hand to catch a cab. Luckily one pulled up right as she walked out of her office, which hardly ever happened around here. She told the driver the address to Luciano's then leaned back in the worn, cab seat while he drove her to the restaurant.

They pulled up about forty minutes later. She was late like she always was but Kaylee didn't seem to care anymore. She used to fuss at them for always being late. Now she had Luciano to keep her company. They were one of those googley-eyed couples that made some people want to puke. Not Tabby. She couldn't wait to have someone look at her the way Luciano looked at Kaylee.

To her surprise Brianna already joined Kaylee at the table. They usually made it about the same time. Either that or Bri would be even later than she would.

"Hey, girl," Brianna shouted across the busy restaurant. She was the boisterous, fun-loving, say-it-like-it-is, one of the group. Kaylee and Brianna each had their apple martinis in front of them with one sitting at the empty seat waiting for her.

"What's up? You're here awfully early tonight," Tabby said as she sat at the table with her friends.

"I thought Kay might be tired of spending all her time with Luciano so I decided to come in a little early to save her," Bri teased.

Kaylee rolled her eyes.

"Please, she probably hoped we wouldn't show," Tabby said. "I'm sure she'd rather spend her time with that gorgeous man of hers rather than us."

"You know I love you both but I'm leaning a bit towards Tabby with this one," Kaylee added in jokingly. "I can't get enough of my Italian Stud."

The three girls all laughed easing the weight off Tabby's chest. This is what she loved about her friends. If she was sad, mad, or lonely they always made her feel better just by being themselves, half the time not even knowing what they were doing. They teased each other, cried with each other, and laughed with each other. Bri and Kaylee were her true sisters.

Tabby lifted her martini glass off the white table cloth and took a drink. Although the restaurant was full, it wasn't overly loud. Almost all the round tables were packed with people enjoying their food, a few couples holding hands and enjoying the romantic atmosphere. She loved this place. With Kaylee marrying Luciano she knew this would be their spot for years to come.

"You know I'm so happy that you're getting married, Kaylee, but you do realize you're making me break my pact again," she told her.

"What pact?" Kaylee and Brianna asked in unison.

"I said I refused to go to another wedding until it was mine, remember? I broke it to go with you to your moms, now I'll have to break it again to be in yours."

"Oh, Tabby, I'm sorry."

"Don't be. You're just lucky I love you so much," Tabby winked at her. "Plus one day you'll both be returning the favor to be in my wedding." She hadn't meant to add that second part. She didn't want this to come back to being about her and what she wanted.

"You know what I think?" Bri asked.

"Here we go again," Kaylee laughed. Bri always tried to give Tabby and Kaylee advice on how to improve their love lives. She didn't understand why. Bri was like Kaylee used to be in some ways, except worse. She never planned on falling in love. Unlike Kaylee's emotional reasons that she'd feared depending on a man, Brianna just didn't want to tie herself down to one man for the rest of her life. She enjoyed her freedom too much for that. She enjoyed men too much. Hell, she was the female version of Nico except she didn't date quite as much.

"What's your goal when it comes to finding a man Tab?" she asked.

"Well Dr. Ruth, like most women I'm looking for Mr. Right, to be swept off my feet, and to fall helplessly in love." It sounded so juvenile when she heard the words in her own ears but they were true. She wouldn't lie to her best friends about that, not that they'd believe her if she tried.

"Exactly," Bri said pointing an accusatory finger at her. "You're always scoping out guys actively looking for Mr. Right. And I hate to break it to you but you don't have the best taste sweetie. You always end up with the kind of men that I want. Someone who is just looking to have a good time instead of someone who wants the same things you do."

Here we go again, Tabby thought. She did this a few months ago with Kaylee that time she actually ended up being right. She didn't want to think about that though.

"I'm tired of seeing you hurt. You're like a magnet for men

who will break your heart." Bri looked at her with a seriousness in her eyes that she didn't often see from her friend.

She hated to hear it but Bri was right. She went after the wrong kind of men and fell too fast, trusted too easily. Nausea swirled in her stomach. She didn't want to be *that* girl. The type that wore their heart on their sleeve and had to continuously put the pieces back together when her heart broke. But then she also couldn't help the way she felt. "I can't change what I want, Bri. I'm not like you. I want a family."

Kaylee grabbed her hand across the table. "No one is telling you to change what you want. You just need to be more careful."

"Maybe I should stay away from men all together," Tabby said sarcastically.

"Blasphemy, child." Brianna smiled then continued, "You're just too trusting. Most men want one thing and one thing only. You need to learn to weed those men out."

"I think Bri might be right," Kaylee added.

"What do you mean, I might be right," Bri jumped in. "Girl, I'm always right. I got you to go for it with Luciano, didn't I?"

"Yeah, whatever…"

Tabby halfway listen to them two women bicker. She hated to admit it but they were right. It wasn't as if she needed a man. She was a strong woman, capable and willing to take care of herself. But the truth was she wanted a good man. Someone to share her life with, her dreams, goals, someone to laugh with, and someone to hold her tight. But the truth is no matter how much she wanted one, she wouldn't let herself settle for anything less than what she deserved. Why she always seemed to attract those kind men she didn't know.

Look at how attracted she was to Nico? He was a nice guy but the wrong kind for her. The one kiss they did share was interrupted by a woman who he was supposed to be meeting for a date that night. Yet she still desired him. *Stupid, stupid, stupid.* On the other hand she could be proud of the fact that she had yet to fall for his flirtatious ways. Want him or not, she

Unexpected Mr. Right

continued to turn him down when he requested a date. Even if it was a struggle. If only he'd stop flirting with her, stop making her so hot things would be so much easier.

"Maybe you guys are right," Tabby said.

"No maybe about it," Bri added.

"I'm just sick and tired of all the losers out there."

"There are good guys out there, Tab. Look at Luciano."

"Yeah, I just don't know how to find them," her voice was playful but her words were very serious.

Before they had a chance to discuss it any further Luciano approached the table, bending down to kiss Kaylee. He pulled two chairs over, one for himself and one for Nico. They always came out and sat with the women, Nico bringing the food on his break and Luciano taking as many moments with his fiancé as he could.

"Nic's coming out in a few minutes, Tabby. You think the two of you can be civil to each other?" Luciano asked.

Ever since he stole the kiss from her in Luciano's office only to be interrupted by a woman, Tabby couldn't seem to get along with him. Although he'd apologized she couldn't bring herself to trust him, which she guessed was a good thing. She didn't seem to have trouble not trusting Nico. Still it bothered her that she was still so upset at him. Sure they'd kissed but it wasn't as if he owed her anything, it wasn't as if they were in a relationship but every time she thought about the woman who he was supposed to date that night, Cindy, her blood boiled. Maybe it was because of all the times she'd been hurt. Cindy could have just as easily been her.

"I don't know, you're asking a lot," she said with a smirk to Luciano. They all knew about the kiss but like Tabby herself they knew it was time she got over it. Nico had no commitment to her just as she didn't have one to him. What they didn't know was at the time, the kiss had meant something to her. Until Cindy walked into the room.

Seconds later Nico approached the table wearing a smile, chef's whites and carrying plates. Tabby sat in the corner trying to ignore the fluttering her in chest.

"Hello, ladies," Nico said setting plates in front of Kaylee, Bri and finally Tabby. "You still mad at me, Slugger?" he said to her with a wink. Embarrassing as it was, she'd smacked Nico after the incident in Luciano's office. Since then he called her Slugger. It was really pretty funny. Well if the name was for someone else it would be.

"What do you think?" It would help if he wasn't so damn fine. She wished anger made her blind. She didn't want to be so attracted to him but one look into his eyes and she wished she were more like Bri, willing to hook up for a night and then forget about him. No guy she ever met had eyes like his. A sinfully dark shade of brown, long, thick soot colored lashes, one look and they could make any woman swoon.

His smile was contagious, big and happy but his face still held a chiseled, strong edge to it. And his body, God she couldn't even imagine what it looked like. He had strong, toned arms and she had no doubt the rest of him was just was delicious. Six feet of yummy, sexy, man. *Yummy, sexy, I never want to settle down, man.* A perfect body wasted on a man that was completely wrong for her.

"You'd think after a couple months you could forgive me. I guess I'm going to have to find a way to make it up to you." She didn't have to guess what he meant by that. Being the fun-loving, flirt he was, Nico always had some kind of sexual innuendo in his words.

"What makes you think you can?"

He bent down and whispered in her ear. The warmth of his breath caused her to shiver. "Why don't you give me a chance to show you what I can do? I promise you, I won't let anyone interrupt us this time."

She couldn't reply. Her mouth felt glued shut. In some ways he was so different from the men she was usually attracted to. She never went for the out-spoken, obvious ladies man type but for some reason, Nico got her juices flowing. She strayed

Unexpected Mr. Right

toward the wolf. Nico let it all out. He didn't try and hide who he was from anyone.

"I don't know what you said over there, Nic but give her a break. She's just might pop you one again." Luciano patted Nico on the back when he spoke.

Everyone laughed. It was a big joke amongst the group but she still felt like shit for hitting him. She'd never slapped anyone else in her life.

Nico backed away from her and sat in the next chair over. "Naw, she's not pissed at me. She's just wants to be."

"You deserve it."

"Tabby," he started to say but looked around as if he remembered they weren't alone. In a quick change of subject he said, "We'll talk later. Dig in everyone. I added a secret ingredient to the sauce tonight."

They ate their meal chatting like always. Tabby worked hard to ignore Nico sitting next to her, to ignore his spicy, sexy scent. The way his leg brushed against hers from time to time, warm, and hard. He made it difficult but she was determined. To keep herself sidetracked she talked about the wedding, making final arrangements. Kaylee and Luciano looked at each other dreamily as Tabby talked their ear off about stuff they already knew.

"Well, I need to get back to work," Nico said standing up.

Luciano stood as well. "We saved this part for as long as we could but since it's obvious the two of you are going to be fighting for sometime we thought you might want to know you're walking together in the wedding."

Kaylee swatted him in the arm. "Nice job breaking it easy."

"Why can't Bri walk with him?" Tabby asked.

"Because she's walking with Marco," Kaylee replied.

"Why can't I walk with Marco?"

"Because—" Kaylee tried to say but Nico broke in.

"Because you're walking with me," he said with an authority she hadn't heard from him before. "We're walking together and that's the end of it." Then he turned and headed into the kitchen. Tabby sat back shocked. Nico was always so easy going. She'd never heard him snap at someone the way he just did her, which made her immediately feel bad for being so foolish. This would be Kaylee and Luciano's day. She could and would put her feelings for Nico aside to make their day a success.

Brianna laughed before downing her Martini. "I guess he told you," she said to Tabby with a smile.

Chapter Two

Nico stalked around the restaurant after hours. They finished everything but he couldn't bring himself to leave. He'd re-cleaned what the waitresses cleaned before leaving, gone through his kitchen to make sure everything was stocked and ready, and he thought about Tabby the whole damn time. The woman was the most irritating person he'd ever met. And the sexiest.

Damn he'd dated a lot of sexy women. Why couldn't he get this one out of his head? To make things worse he hadn't even had her in his bed. She wouldn't give him the time of day and it was seriously starting to piss him off. Sure he liked to flirt but what was the harm in that? Women were beautiful creatures and he liked them to know just how beautiful he thought they were. She acted like that was a crime. He knew how to treat a woman. No one complained before and she wouldn't either if she'd give him a chance.

Plus the last time he checked it wasn't against the law for a single man to go out with different women as long as they all knew the score before hand. He never led anyone on. Right up front he made sure they all knew he wasn't looking to settle down with anyone anytime soon. What was the big deal? He hadn't met a woman who had a problem with him. Until Tabby.

Just forget about her, man. There are plenty of fish in the sea. But he couldn't and he didn't know why. Yeah she was hot, he'd always thought so. He'd flirted with her, asking her out since the first time she came into the restaurant. It became a little game between the two of them, one he enjoyed immensely. Then came the kiss. Nothing had been the same since he had the pleasure of tasting her.

First, she hadn't spoken a civil word to him. He'd had a casual date with another woman that night but canceled to work at the restaurant for Luciano. How was he supposed to know she'd come looking for him? It wasn't as if he had one woman waiting for him while he sat in the boss's office with another. She misunderstood the whole damn thing but Tabby wouldn't hear anything about it.

But the real kicker was himself. Since he'd shared that one kiss with her he hadn't gone out with another woman. Hell, he didn't even look at other women the same way. He couldn't stop thinking about her plump lips beneath his, her smooth, dark skin that he could only dream about exploring. Something was seriously wrong with him. He didn't stress over women, he didn't stalk around the restaurant on a Friday night due to sexual frustration.

Hell, he'd never even experienced sexual frustration before Tabby.

It had to be the fact that she continued to turn him down. He didn't like to sound conceited but women didn't turn him down. It just never happened. Not until Tabitha. Now she hardly spoke a word to him. He missed her gorgeous smile, their easy banter, hell he even missed her turning him down because that meant that they were at least talking. *So what's up, Valenti. You going to sit around and not do anything about it?* He wasn't the type to do nothing. He was an action man, always had been.

Walking over to the register he grabbed the checks for the night. He knew he really shouldn't be doing this but it wasn't as if he was a stalker or anything. *You're just acting like one.* All he needed was her address so he could go see her and talk some damn sense into her. Halfway through the stack he finally came across a check with Tabitha Harris on the top. He quickly scribbled her address down.

"What are you doing, Nic?" Luciano said walking up on him.

Quickly he covered the piece of paper with Tabby's address on it and slid it into his sweaty palm. His heart beat like a teenage boy who'd just been caught with his pants down. "Nothing. Just thought I'd grab the deposit and bring it back to you." He handed the checks and money to Luciano and for the first time in a long actually felt a smile on his face.

Tabby soaked in a warm, lavender bath, a wet rag draped over her eyes. Today was about relaxation. She'd lounged around the house most of the day, watched movies, and thought about her conversation with Bri and Kaylee the night before. After a lot of thought she decided to stop her quest for Mr. Right. At least until she knew exactly what to look for and how to find it. She needed to start slow, take the chance to get to know herself and experience men in a different way than the "husband prospect" she'd always seen them as in the past.

She had to stop falling for the wrong type of men. In reality, she had no idea what men really wanted. Her relationships never lasted long enough for her to find out. Sad, really. A woman who just wanted to love and be loved yet she couldn't keep a relationship? Now that she thought about it, she really never had a real relationship. Not one where they shared the same hopes, dreams. Where she could be herself and share her secrets. Sadly, she tried to be what they all wanted and that wasn't getting her anywhere. How could she be what she didn't understand?

Had she ever actually just been friends with another man? Not that she could remember and that broke her heart. The only people who really loved her for herself were Brianna and Kaylee. They were her closest friends. She'd been an only child with absentee parents who would rather be out on the town attending high society parties than be with her. They'd loved each other, she'd seen it in the way they looked at each other, in the way they touched, the things they did for one another. She however hadn't been good enough.

They'd continually broken her heart since she was a child. Now it seemed something inside her called out to the type of men who would do the same thing. Hurt her. Not love her. The behavior had to stop. Today. Maybe by shifting gears, by putting love on the back burner she could heal like she needed to.

Shifting in the water, Tabby let the bubbles and scents wash away her thoughts about her parents, about her love life. Raising her hand she looked at her pruned fingers and decided it was time to wrap herself in her plush, white robe and slippers and climb on the couch.

Grabbing a towel from the wrack she dried her body before slipping into her robe. As she tied the knot the doorbell sounded in the background. Wiping her hand across the mirror above her sink she glanced at her reflection. Her face was makeup free, her long, black locks tied in a knot on the top of her head. She looked just as relaxed as she felt. Whoever it was would see the laid back version of Tabby.

"Just a minute," she yelled, leaving her slippers behind, padding her bare feet across her carpet. Without checking the peephole she grabbed the handle and cracked the door open. Her breath almost stopped in surprise. Nico stood on the other side.

She couldn't move. All she could do was stand there peaking out of the cracked door. What was he doing here? How did he know where she lived? Against her control her heart rate accelerated with excitement and fear. *Oh God, it's going to be really hard to stay mad at him now.*

"What are you doing here, Nico?" she whispered through the sliver between the wall and door.

"Interrupting something sexy from the looks of it," he said looking her up and down in her robe. Tabby closed the door even more.

Unexpected Mr. Right

"Sounds to me like you were just leaving." When she attempted to close the door, Nico reached out and held it in place.

"Wait. Just let me in, Slugger. We need to talk."

She pulled the door open, slowly, inch by inch all the while arguing with herself internally. *What are you doing? Just tell him you're busy.* "Five minutes," the words slipped out of her mouth. Pushing the door open completely, Nico slid inside, obviously not giving her a chance to change her mind.

"Nice place," he said looking around her large apartment. "It suits you."

Tabby looked around the apartment at her over-stuffed beige couches, at the fireplace lined with matching tiles. It was just the way she wanted it, which was important to her. She'd never been allowed to decorate her own room as a child. It was all about her mom and Mom wanted the whole house to coordinate in some way. The ideas of a child didn't go with her theme. "Thanks. I worked hard on it."

"That's what you do isn't it?" he asked. She knew he was just making conversation. They'd talked about their jobs a hundred times before at Luciano's.

"Yeah. That's what I do." Tabby pointed to her couch, "Have a seat. I doubt you came over here to talk about my career and your five minutes is winding down." *Why are you being so harsh with him? So he was casually dating another woman when you kissed. It's not as if he had any commitment to you.*

"You ever going to get over being pissed at me?" he asked sitting down.

"I'm not pissed. I just don't want to play the game anymore. What's the point in the flirting and you asking me out every time we see each other when we both know it would never work out anyway." There, she finally said it. She finally let him know the score.

"Sweetheart, that's who I am. I flirt, I like to have fun. There's nothing wrong with that. Besides, I think you enjoy it a lot more than you're willing to admit."

He was right. She did enjoy their joking, all the winks, and sexy smiles he always sent her way. It felt fun and forbidden but she couldn't admit that to him. "You're full of yourself," she took a seat on the other couch that sat across from his. "Maybe I just didn't want you to feel bad? Maybe I was letting you down easily." *There. How do you like that?*

He turned into suave mode right in front of her. His dark, sexy, bedroom eyes taking her in. "I know women, Slugger. No one kisses someone the way you kissed me when you're letting them down easily."

Tabby stuttered, real words escaping her but only for a minute. "You're awful cocky. Maybe you think your player status is a good thing but I don't find it amusing."

"I can show you amusing."

She stood up annoyed. "You're a piece of work you know that? I think your five minutes is up and for the record I do know how to have fun." She turned to walk towards the door but stopped when she heard him exhale a heavy, frustrated breath. His eyes held a different tone than she usually saw from him. He was so carefree and right now he looked like his mind was heavy.

After running a hand through his short hair he spoke. "Listen, I didn't come over here to fight with you. I came over to apologize again for what happened a few months ago. I'd canceled my date and didn't expect her to come to the restaurant that night. I'm really not the deviant you seem to think I am."

Tabby sat back on the couch. Guilt washed over her. He really didn't do anything wrong. It was her own hang-ups that made her so angry with him. She hated the feeling of knowing she expelled that onto him. "I guess I should apologize for being such a bitch lately. I shouldn't have made such a big deal of things."

A smile graced his face. "Before you forgive me, I'm saying I'm sorry for us being interrupted and for how that made you feel but I'm not apologizing for the kiss. That part I meant."

She didn't know what came over her but the words filled her head and she let them escape her lips. "I didn't ask you to."

Unexpected Mr. Right   23

When his smile grew she added, "But that doesn't mean it will happen again."

"Why not give me a chance? All I want is a date, not a lifetime commitment."

"You ever stop to think that maybe a commitment is what I'm looking for? When I go out with someone I want to know there's a possibility of a future, not just a good time." They'd played cat and mouse enough, skirting around the issues without laying it all on the line and now she knew she needed to do just that. Then maybe he'd stop asking her out, making it harder and harder to deny him each time.

The silence stretched on, proving her point even more. They wanted two different things so what was the point in playing the game? The longer they sat there staring at each other she felt the need to make another excuse for herself. The need came out of nowhere and she couldn't explain it but she didn't want him to think she was some clingy woman who just needed a man. Plus she'd just decided to make some changes, didn't she? "Even if that wasn't the case, I'm not dating right now, Nico."

"Why not?"

She didn't want to go into the whole story with him. It was a little embarrassing to admit all her heartaches of the past. "I have some things I need to figure out. Until then I don't really want to have any kind of sexual relationship with a man." He seemed so confused she couldn't help but laugh.

"What's so funny?" He asked obviously not feeling her humor.

"You're acting like someone just took away your favorite toy. You have so many women lining up to go out with you that you don't need me."

The look vanished replaced by his predatory stare. "How does someone know a favorite toy that they've never had the pleasure to play with?"

Her laughter stopped. "You're proving my point further, Nico."

"No, I'm joking. Lighten up. I have a solution to our

problem."

Tabby leaned back in her cushioned couch waiting for him to continue.

"Even though you're such a grouch," he said the words playfully. "I like hanging out with you. We used to all have fun together on Friday nights. So, since I'm such a fiend and you don't want to go out with me, can't we just spend some time together as friends? No pressure, no promises, just a couple friends hanging out from time to time."

"Why would you want to do that? What's in it for you?"

"You know, I am capable of spending time with a woman without trying to get into her pants. We always got along well, what's wrong with us becoming better friends?"

Tabby sat there not answering, thinking about what he said. It was perfect, really. He didn't realize it but Nico had just given her a chance to prove herself. She didn't want to think of herself as the type of woman who always fell for the wrong men. By spending extra time with Nico she could prove to herself that she could become close to him without risking her heart. And maybe she could get some insight into how men like Nico thought. She might learn something about herself in the process.

But what about Kay and Bri? If she started spending any time with Nico outside of Friday nights no one would believe it was just about being friends. They'd worry about her, be afraid she would fall for him and end up getting hurt. The idea of spending time with him was too appealing. This was the right decision. She felt it deep within her heart. She'd never had a really close male friend before. And she liked him, as much as she didn't like to admit it. He was fun and made her laugh.

The only hard part would be keeping it from Bri and Kay. She hated the idea of lying to them, she told them everything but she really wanted to have a close guy friend in her life and she didn't think they'd understand. How could they? They were both so different than she was. So much stronger. She wanted to be that strong too.

"Are you sure this isn't just a ploy, Nico?"

"Yeah, I know a lost cause when I see one," he said with a smile.

"Then we have a deal. The only thing is I don't want to tell Kaylee, Brianna or Luciano." She felt foolish wanting to hide this from her friends but this is something she was doing just for herself. She had a lot of things to figure out and this was the best way.

"You embarrassed of me, Slugger?" Nothing seemed to faze him. He took everything with a light, happy smile.

"A little bit." She couldn't help but give him a hard time. See if she could get a rise out of him.

"Was that a joke, Tabby? I'm so proud of you."

"Well someone has to be serious around you since you never are."

"Two in a row. How'd I get so lucky?" He seemed to be enjoying himself. She suddenly was too but she also wanted to make sure he knew she was serious.

"Kay and Bri won't understand. If they see us spending time together they'll assume it's romantic and that I'm going to get my heart broken. I don't want to argue with them about it." She stopped for a minute before she continued, "plus, it's a little exciting to have a secret no one knows about, isn't it?"

Nico laughed. "I think you're more of a bad girl than you want people to think." Mischief danced across his brown eyes. "Sure, I'll keep your secret."

Nico left Tabby's apartment a short time later pissed as hell at himself. *What the hell was that?* He still couldn't believe what he'd said. Not that it was bad to be friends with her but it wasn't like him to beg for a woman's attention and that's what he felt like he did. She was right when she said there were plenty of other women who wanted him so why the hell was he making plans to be *friends* with a woman who didn't want to give him the time of day.

He didn't know where the crazy idea came from. All he knew was the words had somehow sneaked out of his mouth and she'd agreed. He couldn't for the life of him figure out why he was pursuing a woman who kept shooting him down, but he was. Actually, scratch that, he knew what it was. He liked a challenge, always had and Tabby was a challenge. It wasn't often that women challenged him. And no matter what she said, he knew she was interested.

He saw it in her eyes, the way she looked at him when she didn't know he was looking. She took things way too seriously and he wanted to be the one to loosen her up, to show her a good time. He knew a wildcat crouched beneath the surface, he just had to lure her out. He liked that. Liked her.

Not enough to propose marriage or start picking out china patterns and that's what she seemed to want. Mr. Dependable, boring, white picket fence kind of man and that wasn't him. The just friend's idea really was the best route. Hopefully they'd move to friends with benefits. Why try and be anything more? They'd be doomed from the start.

So now he had to figure out what men and women did together when they were just friends. Dinner? Movies? Concerts? Did men still take women to do those kinds of things when they weren't sleeping together? *Pretty sad you don't know the answer to this, man.* He'd never not known what to do with a woman before. He knew how to flirt with them, seduce them, and give them pleasure, all the while making sure they knew the score. Fun and sex, that's all he had to offer. Well, all he ever wanted to offer at least.

When he first walked in her apartment all he had on his mind was pleasure and sex. She always looked gorgeous but knowing she was probably naked under her white robe almost did him in. Her tall, dark body looked delectable in white. It took all the strength he had not to reach for the ties and unwrap her, inch by delicious inch.

It was the first time he'd seen her not completely put together. Her hair wasn't styled, her make-up wasn't in place but none of it took away from her beauty. In fact, it made her even more desirable. Her plump lips didn't need color to draw his attention to them. They were kissable enough as is. Her eyes were just as beautiful. Their greenish-brown tone drew him in every time.

Which is why you find yourself in trouble. She had him hard as nails without trying. For the first time in his life he was abstinent and it was because he only wanted one woman. She had him out of his element and he had to figure out what the hell to do about it. But he knew he'd figure it out. He always did. Tabby wasn't any different.

Chapter Three

Nico still hadn't called but Tabby didn't let it bother her. She didn't expect anything from him. If he decided he wanted to spend some time together than she'd be up for it, if not, that would be cool too. She didn't want to stress too much on it. There would always be another way for her to experiment. The way she saw it, he probably realized it was too much work to try and build a friendship with her. They'd see each other tomorrow night at Luciano's and he'd probably call off the whole thing.

As soon as she got home from work she went in and changed into her light blue Juicy pants and a tight, but comfortable t-shirt. Her newly cut hair loosely framed her face at the chin. It had been a major decision for her to cut her locks. Years of growth littered the beauty shop floor but she liked the change.

Now she was home, relaxed and needed to get some substance in her stomach. Preferably something delicious and fattening. Tabby walked into her kitchen and opened the fridge. She pushed the yogurt out of the way, ignored the chicken salad leftovers from the night before then closed the door. Even though her stomach growled, nothing she had tempted her.

She took a couple steps towards the frosted glass doors on the other side of her kitchen marked Pantry when the phone rang. "Hello," she said holding the cordless to her head while she continued her quest for food.

"I have homemade chicken parmesan, pasta, and wine. The only thing I'm missing is someone to share it with. You interested?" Nico's smooth voice echoed through the phone putting a smile on her face. He was offering food. Exactly what she needed.

"I'd do just about anything if you'd feed me." Tabby sat on the white, wooden barstools in her kitchen, no longer interested in anything she had in her pantry.

"Do I really get to feed you? Now that would be a good time."

Oh God, he never stopped. Switching the phone to her left ear she asked, "I thought we were working on being friends".

"This friendship thing is all kind of new to me, Slugger. You mean to tell me you, Bri and Kaylee don't sit around feeding each other? Damn, I'm going to have to rethink this whole friend thing." He said in his usual playful tone.

"I didn't say that." She didn't know what came over her but she wanted to be just as playful as him. This wasn't about love or relationships so she didn't have to worry about taking it too seriously. She'd never been much of a flirt with the men she went out with. She wanted them to know she was looking for something permanent, not just a flirtatious fling. "You're being awful quiet, Nico. I think this is the only time I've heard you at a loss for words."

He laughed. "It takes more than that to make me at a loss for words. I was just taking a minute to imagine a visual."

She was so out of her league trying to match Nico's teasing nature. But she'd work on it. Tabby didn't like not excelling at everything she tried to do. That included friendly flirting with Nico. As long as he knew it was only friendly and not sexual. "I thought it was pretty good. Isn't that supposed to be a guy's biggest fantasy? Women together."

"It's one of them, that's for sure. And I didn't say it wasn't hot, I just said it takes more than that to make me speechless."

"I'd imagine that's because you have so much experience

with flirtatious women? I think you're somewhat of an expert on the subject."

"Ouch. You're always busting my balls, Slugger. I think you're somewhat an expert on *that* subject."

"Whatever," Tabby said trying to hold back her smile. "Just get over here with my food. I'm starving."

"Be careful what you say. I can take that a couple different ways."

Tabby hung up the phone and headed towards the bathroom. She wanted to run a quick comb through her hair before Nico arrived. She didn't bother to change her clothes because hey, it was just Nico. If Kaylee or Bri were coming over she wouldn't change from her lounging clothes. Why should Nico be any different? Tabby curled up on her couch, her legs under her. Picking up the remote she flipped through the channels absent mindedly. Should she have tried to flirt with Nico on the phone earlier? The last thing she wanted was for him to get the wrong idea. She couldn't think about anything more than a harmless friendship with him.

She already liked him more than she should. Not that she was falling for him or anything, but he did make her laugh a lot. He was fun, outgoing, determined and seemed to like her. That was dangerous grounds. If she let herself get too wrapped up in this whole friendship thing, when he lost interest, she'd be the one left hurting. That was the opposite reason she decided to go along with all of this.

And he would lose interest. From what she saw of his other relationships, he always did. Usually pretty darn quickly too. *Have I ever seen him with a woman more than once or twice?* He was a confirmed bachelor and from what she could tell he liked that life. He was so different than her. Maybe that's what made him feel so exciting. Exciting didn't last a lifetime though. Dependable and serious, that's what lasted for the long haul.

Tabby got up and lit the cinnamon candles on her fireplace. She loved relaxing in the evening with candles lit around her room. Just like with her baths, it put her at ease. She loved

Unexpected Mr. Right

different scents and the calming flutter of candle flames. Her home was littered with different candles, the scents and colors matching each room.

A knocked sounded at the door while she stood losing herself in the red and gold of the flame. She glanced at her watch. It had only been a few minutes since they got off the phone. He must live close by to have arrived so quickly. For the first time since he came over last week she wondered how he knew where she lived that first night. She hadn't thought to ask him before. She knew Kay wouldn't have told him without warning her first. Bri might just for fun but she would have eventually told her. Or at least asked how it went.

Her friends didn't trust her to make decisions for herself so she doubted either of them really would have given him her address. They treated her like she was fragile, like she would break if treated badly. It was because they loved her but she didn't want to be seen as weak. She wanted to prove to herself and to them as well that she was stronger than they thought.

Nico knocked again. Tabby walked over, this time peaking through her peephole to make sure it was him before she opened the door. His short, black hair was tousled on his head like he hadn't taken the time to comb it, but it didn't take away from his appeal. He was dressed in a pair of loose fitting jeans that rode low on his hips and a white t-shirt.

Before she had the chance to greet him, he spoke. "You cut your hair," he said reaching out his free hand to touch her hair.

Tabby gestured for him to come in. When he did she closed and locked the door behind him. "Yep. Just today."

"What made you do that?" he asked.

She gave him a don't-go-there look, "Don't ever ask a woman that, Nico. Just smile and tell her she looks great." Tabby led the way to the kitchen with Nico not far behind.

"Ah, but I didn't know if you'd take that the wrong way since we're working on just being friends. I told you I'm still learning about this. See, if I was picking you up for a date I'd tell you how well the shorter length frames your face. How sexy it is when you turn and this strand," he grabbed her hair and pushed it behind her ear, "falls in front of your eyes bringing out the different colors and making me notice how round and welcoming they are. I'd tell you how it brings more attention to your plump, kissable lips making it damn hard to keep from tasting them."

Tabby sat in the chair before her legs gave out beneath her.

"But since we're just friends I wasn't sure if I was allowed to tell you all that."

Damn he's good. She looked at him trying to hold in her smile. He didn't bother, his right side rose in a crooked grin. "I'll make an exception this time," she tried to hide the tremble in her voice, "since you're still learning and all".

Nico set the brown paper bag containing their dinner on her kitchen counter. The first thing he noticed was like her living room, her kitchen was spotless. Second, that it suited her. He could tell she spent a lot of time decorating her home, making everything just right. The room was colored a dark green and cranberry. Everything matched, with not a lot of clutter. He could do some serious cooking here. Nothing felt as good as messing up a neat kitchen. Maybe he'd get to mess hers up. She needed a little bit of mess in her life.

"Where are the plates?" he asked after pulling the food from the bag. "I'll also need wine glasses and a corkscrew."

He watched her walk around the kitchen grabbing what he asked for, her hips swaying in the process. She was a slender woman, but she did have a few curves and they were all in the right places. Damn he wanted her. It was going to be tough to stick with the whole friend's thing but he'd gone and opened his mouth. Now there wasn't anything to do but follow through with it.

Even if he didn't understand why they were doing it. They wanted each other. He could see in her eyes that she wanted him just as much as he wanted her. Nico knew women well but he'd didn't understand them. They were both consenting adults. What was the problem with sating their desire for one another? They'd both go into it knowing he wasn't the kind of man for a serious relationship so how could she get hurt if she knew the score?

Tabby handed him two plates. Using the utensils he brought along he dished food out on each of the two plates while she grabbed wine glasses and a corkscrew. "I hope you like red wine," he asked her when she set the glasses down in front of him.

"Yes, I do."

"I thought about bringing you apple martinis but I thought maybe we'd try something different. You'll have your martinis tomorrow."

She laughed. "We are predictable, aren't we?"

"No, you? Not that I'm complaining. I like that you spend your Friday nights at Luciano's." He started to pour their drinks.

"If not, Kay and Luciano would have never met."

"Neither would we. And look, we're starting to build such a great friendship too. You can't forget about that." He didn't. His body hadn't been able to forget her since that very first Friday night months ago.

"No, we can't forget about that. Otherwise I wouldn't have this delicious meal in front of me," her eyes sparkled and a smile graced her plump lips.

"I see how you are. Just use me for my food. What do I get in return?"

"My friendship. That's what you're looking for, isn't it?"

He winked at her. "I'm looking for whatever you will give me, Slugger."

She smacked his arm teasingly. "Stop with the sweet talk and let's eat."

"Anyone ever tell you, you can be damn bossy when you want to be?" He liked that about her. It made things a little more interesting. Nico picked up the plates and brought them over to the small table in her kitchen. He noticed her apartment came with at formal dining room but thought they'd feel much more comfortable in her kitchen. He didn't want things to be formal. What he really wanted was wild, carefree, fun, sweaty sex but he knew he wouldn't get that. Not yet.

Tabby wanted friendship so that's what she would get. Of course if she changed her mind he could do that too. Well. He took a seat placing a plate in front of two of the four chairs at the table. Tabby was right behind with their glasses filled halfway with the deep red wine.

"This looks great, Nico." She grabbed forks and knives out of a drawer then took the chair across from him.

He watched as her long, slender fingers grasped utensils. She cut into the chicken mixing it with a small fork full of pasta and took a bite. *I've never wanted to be a fork so much in my life*, he thought as she sensually pulled the utensil from her sexy lips. She didn't do it on purpose. He knew that. Hell, she probably didn't know he was getting a hard on under the table just from watching her eat. But he was. Just like a damn teenager he was growing hard just by watching a sexy woman enjoy her meal.

"Mmmm. This is orgasmic. I was even hungrier than I thought." Her words made him pulse behind his zipper. As if realizing what she just said, Tabby put a hand up to her mouth like she could erase the words with her fingers. "I didn't mean…oh God, can we forget I just brought up orgasms at the table. That's the last thing I need on my mind."

He liked the idea of Tabby having orgasms on her mind. They sure as hell were on his. "If you're thinking about orgasms maybe we should do something about it. If you think my cooking is good, the man behind the spatula is even better."

She shivered. From across the table he could see her body quake slightly. He wanted to do more than just make her shiver. He wanted to make her come. Over and over again. *Just friend's remember?* Yeah right. Since the first time he laid eyes on her he wanted to be more than friends with her. He wanted her.

"I don't have orgasms on the brain."

"I was worried that I wouldn't be able to keep our conversation away from sex. I'm surprised, and excited that you're the one who brought it up." If she agreed they could do more than just talk about it.

"Please. You're reachin'. I didn't bring up sex. It's a figure of speech."

"Well I *figure* you and I being together is inevitable. You're just delaying the process."

Her body felt the same way. He was fine and every time she looked at him she couldn't help but imagine what it would be like to be with him. The way women flocked around him, the way they looked at him he had to have something special between the sheets. Too bad she didn't go into sex lightly because her body wanted nothing more than to experience him. "You're determined."

"When I want something."

"I thought you wanted to be friends?"

"We can still be friends and enjoy one another. There aren't any rules against that."

Maybe not to him but to her, there were. She knew what she wanted and non-commitment sex wasn't what she had in mind. For now she didn't want anything, no men at all. Eventually, she'd find the one, a man who would commit to her wholeheartedly. "I'll stick to just friends. I wouldn't want to deny all the other women of San Francisco the chance to be with the famed Nico Valenti." She said the words meaning them to be a joke but by the look in his eyes Nico didn't agree with her humor.

"There you go busting my balls again. I'm not that bad, you know?"

"I saw the writing on the bathroom wall in Luciano's."

He looked stunned but then surprised her when he said, "Well I hope it was at least something good."

She envied his easy-going, fun personality. He took

everything in stride. Would he really not care if someone wrote about his sexual activities in a public place? "You are so bad, Nico. No one wrote about you on the wall. Not yet at least."

"Are you threatening me, Tabby? If you are I think you should at least test me out. You know, so you know what to write when you do," he said with his easy going smile.

"Oh, I already know what to write."

"And how's that?" he looked intrigued.

"Women's intuition, Nico. Women's intuition." She downed a drink of her wine, then smiled.

They finished their meal with easy conversation and a few more laughs along the way. Tabby was amazed at how comfortable she felt around him. Sure they'd known one another for months now but only within the walls of Luciano's and the majority of the time with Bri, Kaylee and Luciano as company as well. They'd never been alone together as long as they were tonight but she found she enjoyed it. She felt at ease with him. Probably because she didn't go into it expecting anything more than friendship.

Normally when she had dinner with a man it was with the prospect of something more, something serious. With Nico they were just two friends hanging out. She felt as if she would spending time with Brianna, Kaylee or even Luciano. Like she could be herself. She didn't have to impress anyone. Because of this, she didn't want it to end. "Do you want to go sit on the balcony for a little while? We can have another glass of wine."

"Sure," Nico replied standing up, grabbing their wine glasses in one hand, the bottle in his other one.

Waves of delight swept through her. Having Nico as a friend felt good. Her mind and body felt so loose and calm spending time with a man without wondering, wishing if he was the one for her. This was the best choice she could have made for herself. For once she wasn't thinking of her future, just living in the moment. "The sliding glass door is off the living room.

Unexpected Mr. Right   **37**

Go ahead and go out. I need to grab a sweatshirt."

She watched him walk through the kitchen, stepping out seconds later. "Take your time," Nico called after her when she started to walk down the hall towards her bedroom.

"I'll be just a minute." She stepped into her room leaving him alone, closing the door behind her. Tabby took the time to quickly brush her teeth in the bathroom connected to her bedroom. Not that she'd be kissing anyone tonight but she still didn't want to fire garlic breath at him when they talked either. Then she walked over to her antique dresser and pulled out one of her comfy, warm sweatshirts and put it on.

What would Brianna and Kaylee think if they knew she would be lounging on her balcony, sipping wine and chatting with Nico tonight? Of course they'd support her no matter what. She knew her friends loved her and liked Nico a lot but they still wouldn't trust her not to get her heart involved. They loved her so much they would worry she'd end up hurt, that she couldn't keep herself from falling for him because they knew how much she wanted her happily ever after.

This time was different. Going into a friendship knowing the man involved wasn't for her was different than going into a relationship praying that he would be her soul mate.

Running a hand through her newly cropped hair she went to join Nico on the balcony. He sat in one of her white chairs leaning back, his feet propped on one of the spare chairs.

"You have a lot of white stuff." He pulled out her chair for her and she sat down.

"I do?" She'd never really noticed before.

"Yep. White chairs here, in your kitchen, your carpet, the sexy little robe you wore the other night."

She wanted to say "so" but she didn't. What he meant by this she had no clue. "I like white. Is there anything wrong with that?"

"No. I just didn't know you were so vanilla."

"Hey. I'm not vanilla." They weren't talking about ice cream here and they both knew it but she continued with the analogy anyway. "I'll have you know I can be just as chocolate or rocky road as the next girl."

He had the gall to laugh. Then he leaned his chair back so it sat on the back legs only. "You are so are no rocky road. Maybe vanilla with a couple sprinkles on top but that's as crazy as you get."

He baited her and she knew it. Unfortunately should couldn't keep herself from taking said bait. "Well maybe I'll have to find a way to show you I'm not vanilla with sprinkles."

"Maybe you will." His cocky tone said it all. She walked right into a trap set by a master hunter.

"What are you going to do to prove it to me?"

Well she hadn't thought that far. This flirtatiousness wasn't her style so now she didn't know what to do or say. She couldn't do what he wanted her to do which was no doubt something out of character for her, like kiss him or something. At a loss, and a little miffed about it she said, "I have no idea."

Nico shook his head a small chuckle slipping from his lips. "Maybe one day, Slugger. Here, I poured you another glass." He handed her a glass of wine.

She had a feeling for some reason he wanted to let her off easy. Thankfully she took his out. "Thanks. Dinner was great. I wish I could cook like that."

"You don't cook?"

"I do, but not very well. Most of my meals consist of take-out or something I can throw together easily."

"Not your thing?"

"I don't know if that's really what it is or just the fact that I've never taken the time to learn." As an adult she never learned because she didn't have anyone to cook for besides herself. What was the fun in that?

"You're mom never taught you?" He sounded shocked but that didn't surprise her. From what Kaylee said he and Luciano came from a very close knit family.

"She didn't have time."

"What's your excuse now?"

"I guess I don't have one. Just haven't learned."

Nico shook his head at her. "That's a crime. You're going to

Unexpected Mr. Right   **39**

have to let me show you how."

"What would you show me? Cooking for one?" she snickered when she spoke.

"No smart-aleck. I'd just show you some of the basics. Teach you how to make a few things. Cooking for one is no different than cooking for more besides the fact that you're cooking less." She looked over at him. "And if you're looking for someone to cook for there's always me."

"Cooking for a chef?"

"Even chefs need a break."

She shrugged her shoulders not letting her excitement show. Who wouldn't want to learn to cook like Nico? "Sure sounds like fun."

His voice lowered an octave. "I can promise you it will be a good time. That's my specialty."

"Showing women a good time is your specialty? I'm not sure you should be bragging about that."

"You give me a hard time but you're the one who always has her mind in the gutter. First orgasms, now this. I was talking about cooking." He winked at her.

He excelled at turning things around. Everything she said he turned into something sexual but he made it so she felt she was the one who couldn't stop thinking about jumping into bed. She smiled internally at his antics. He was right, she did need to lighten up. When she did she realized she actually enjoyed this little back and forth game they played. "Did you take a flirting 101 class or are you this good on your own?"

He shrugged his shoulders. "I'm just this good on my own, Slugger."

"I really wish you'd stop calling me that." Every time he did the nickname reminded her how horrible she'd been to him.

"I could always call you the Great Bambino if you preferred."

"The great who?" She had no idea who that was but the name didn't sound much better than Slugger.

"Babe Ruth. They used to call him the Great Bambino."

"Let me get this straight, you either want to name me after

an old baseball player or a ten year old boy. Now I see what you really think of me."

Nico laughed. "Believe me. I know you're a woman. That isn't something I'm likely to forget."

Chapter Four

No way could he forget her feminine appeal. Especially when she looked at him the way she was right now. Her big eyes wide with shock and desire. He didn't understand her shock. She knew him well enough to know he wanted her and he wouldn't shy away from admitting it. Hell, he'd remind her every chance he had. That's just the way he was. And she liked it. She may not want to admit it but she did. He could see it in her eyes, in the way the pulse in her throat beat rapidly, the way her hands shifted nervously. God he wanted this woman. Every sassy, sexy inch of her.

"I feel bad."

"Feel bad about what?" he asked.

"Hitting you. I never should have done that. Not that I'm looking for an excuse but it happened in the heat of the moment. I'm sorry."

She sipped a drink of her wine. Nico watched her pink tongue sneak out and lick a stray drop off her lip. *Oh yeah. He knew she was a woman alright.* He lifted his eyes from her lips before he did something stupid like kiss her. They were finally starting to make some headway and he knew enough to know kissing her would be a bonehead move on his part. "Don't feel bad. There are plenty of times in my life I probably deserved to be slapped and never was. You can say you're the lucky woman who got the privilege of the job."

"Yeah but you didn't deserve it that time."

"No I didn't. But don't worry. I'll let you make it up to me." He couldn't wait.

Tabby walked into Luciano's the following Friday. The night before, Nico left her apartment not long after she finished apologizing for smacking him. It felt good to get it off her chest. Even if he continued to call her Slugger, which knowing Nico he would, she felt better having talked to him about it. She held guilt about it since the day it happened.

Kaylee already sat at the table sipping a water when she walked in. "Hey, girl."

"Hey. How ya been? Anything new?"

Tabby automatically shuffled her hands nervously. Kaylee asked an innocent question but her guilt made sweat bead on her forehead regardless. She never was the best at keeping secrets. Especially from her best friends. Was she suspicious of anything? Did she know? Questions clouded her brain and kept her from answering. She knew if she opened her mouth something stupid would come out.

"Hello? Is everything okay?" Kaylee asked waving a hand in front of Tabby's face.

"Sorry. Just spacing. I had a long day at work."

Kaylee looked concerned but didn't say anything. Thank God for small favors. She didn't know if she could flat out lie to her friends. Right now at least she was only lying by omission. *Like that's any better.* Tabby pulled out her chair and sat down. It's not like what she was doing was a big deal. But then, they might not see it as hanging with a friend, not with Nico's or her own track record with dating.

"I guess we better be glad it's Friday then."

"You can say that again," just as Tabby finished her sentence Bri sat down at the table.

"I'm sure as hell glad it's Friday. Now where are our martinis?" Bri asked with a smile.

Unexpected Mr. Right   **43**

"I don't know but I need one." Tabby felt strange about tonight. She wasn't sure how to act around Nico. Well she knew how she should act, normal. It's not as if anything happened with them but she still felt a little weird. Maybe because there was a big secret between the two of them that no one else knew. That had to be it. As if their waiter read her mind he came out with their martinis. Tabby drank half of hers in one quick gulp.

"Um, you okay over there? You're drinking like a college girl at a dorm party." Bri gave her a curious look.

"I'm fine. Like I said it's been a long day." *Plus I spent half of last night flirting, eating and drinking wine with Nico and I can't tell you about it. Still I don't know why I'm tripping. All I did is spend time with a friend.* That's what they agreed on and that's all they did.

"If you say so. Hey, here comes the Italian Stud," Bri pointed across the restaurant to Luciano. That quickly, the conversation switched. Luciano joined them at the table. Not too much longer and Nico would be out as well. Goosebumps pebbled on her skin at the thought. She looked forward to Friday's at Luciano's, the way they were before she started being such a bitch to him. Now they could spend time together like they used to, laughing and talking without tension clouding the air. Tension she caused but that was besides the point.

"Hello, Bella." Luciano kissed Kaylee before sitting down. "Ladies," he tilted his head toward Bri and Tabby.

"You two are disgustingly in love," Brianna pointed to the couple. "Shouldn't you be over the kissy-face stage by now?"

"No!" Tabby answered for them. "You should never get over that stage. Kissing is one of the most sensual ways to show your affection for someone. When I'm with someone I never tire of kissing them." Nico happened to walk up just as she finished speaking.

"You see, now there's something we have in common, Slugger. I've been told I'm an exceptional kisser," his dimple shown when he stretched his mouth into a seductive smile.

"Are you forgetting I've had experience with your kissing

first hand?" she asked deciding to be a little playful. She really felt so much better being friends with him again. She didn't want to admit it but she'd missed not having to act mad when he flirted with her.

"No way could I forget that. I was just trying to see if you agreed." He set plates in front of her friends. When he did Tabby realized they weren't alone. How could she have forgotten that? Brianna, Kaylee and even Luciano looked at her like she had four eyes popping out of her head.

"What the hell? Did I step into the twilight zone?" Bri asked. "Normally you'd be biting his head off by now."

Oops. Tabby didn't know how to respond to her friend. Should she tell them about that chat and that they made up? That might lead into territory she didn't want to cover so instead of saying anything she took another drink of her martini.

Obviously seeing her distress, Nico saved her by responding. "Tab and I came to a mutual agreement. We're right as rain."

"Well halle-freaking-lujah." Brianna clapped her hands.

"Leave me alone you, bully," Tabby teased. "I wasn't that bad to him."

"You weren't the nicest, Sweetie," Kaylee added. They were the only two people in the world who could tell her like it is and she knew it came from the heart. And she knew they were right. Her comment reiterated how unfairly she treated Nico, making her feel bad all over again. He was right. She really did need to figure out a way to make it up to him. Just not the way he wanted her too.

"Well, we're fine now," Nico sat next to her at the table.

"Yeah, I can see that," Brianna added.

Okay, time to change the subject. Tabby didn't want to give her friends the chance to ask any questions. "I bet your mom is getting so excited for the wedding, Kaylee." They'd just begun to rebuild their relationship around the time Kaylee finally admitted that she was in love with Luciano. In fact, seeing her mother fall in love had enabled Kaylee to finally go for what she wanted, Luciano.

Her question provided the perfect distraction as Kaylee began to talk about her mom and then the wedding. Without being obvious, Tabby sneaked a quick glance at Nico. He offered a wink telling her he knew what she was up to. Try as she might she couldn't hold in her smile. He always seemed to do that to her.

"What's the smile for? You look like you're up to something," Bri said with suspicion.

Yeah, she really sucked at this incognito thing. Not only that but all of a sudden Brianna decided to turn into Magnum PI. "Nothing. You know how much I love weddings. I'm just excited to hear if Kaylee and Luciano have made any more decisions." Tabby took a bite of the Italian sausage off her plate.

Brianna didn't look convinced. If she kept it up, she'd just tell her what was going on. It's not as if she was doing anything wrong anyway. They'd have to learn to trust that she wouldn't get her heart involved, that she wouldn't get hurt.

"You know no one makes any decisions about this wedding unless you're involved. You're our wedding extraordinaire."

"I am not."

"Are to," Bri countered.

Finally Nico broke in. "All right kids. Stop bickering before we have to put the two of you in time out. I don't have long to visit tonight."

Bri looked hesitant but she let the subject drop. They finished their food and talked about Luciano and Kaylee's big day.

"How'd you get Tabby to forgive you?" Luciano asked when they walked out of the restaurant that night. Before he and Kaylee got together they used to hang out after Luciano's closed and have a beer. Now Luciano has his beautiful fiancé to go home to. He rushed like a mad man to get out of there.

Nico was so happy for his cousin. He'd prayed for years he'd find a woman as wonderful as Kaylee to be happy with.

"I just threw some of the Valenti charm at her," he teased. "If you want, I could give you some lessons."

Luciano shot him a look that said he didn't think Nico was the slightest bit funny. "I'm the one going home to a beautiful woman tonight while if my calculations are correct you haven't had a date since your big blow up with Tabby."

Shit. He'd hoped no one noticed that. "I haven't found anyone new who has perked my interest. Don't go reading something into nothing." That's all he needed. He'd given Luciano a hard time about Kaylee a few months before but that situation was different. They were in love. Luciano wanted more than the life he led, he just hadn't known it. Nico didn't.

Luciano stopped him before they went their separate ways. "Just be careful, buddy. If you are up to anything, if there's more to your sudden truce than you're letting on, be careful. Tabby's looking for that happily ever after and if you aren't, I'm afraid she'll get hurt."

Damn. Why did everyone think he was such an asshole? He'd never broken a woman's heart in the past. What made Luciano think he would start now? He knew Nico always make sure the women he dated knew up front that he didn't want a relationship. Why did his own cousin think he would change the rules of the game now by letting Tabby think he wanted anything more than what he did?

She knew what he wanted. A good time, friendship and a little nookie. She denied him the nookie so they had the friendship and the good times. What was wrong with that? "She's not going to get hurt. We're friends. That's all. There isn't anything going on that wasn't before."

Luciano nodded at him. "I just had to say it, Nic. She's Kaylee's best friend and I'd hate for a rift to come between us all."

He started to feel guilty and he didn't know why. He hadn't touched Tabby but not for lack of trying. She was a good woman. Hurting her was the last thing on his mind and he thought he'd been doing a good job until now. Would she take his flirtations the wrong way? Would a friendship mean more to her than she was letting on? He didn't think so. She seemed really intent on this friendship thing.

And so was he. Sure he'd like to have a night or two with her but he also liked being friends with her. Last he checked he wasn't breaking any laws. They wouldn't go anywhere that she didn't want to go. He'd never lie to her. Didn't his cousin know that? Was he really the bad guy Tabby, and now Luciano, seemed to think him? Now he started to doubt himself and that didn't sit well. "Don't worry, cousin. I'm on my best behavior." Nico turned and walked away.

Next time he saw Tabby he'd make sure she knew where things stood, he wasn't the relationship kind of guy and never would be.

"Here kitty, kitty, kitty." Tabby called to her Siamese cat, Charming. He came running into the kitchen at the sound of her voice. She fed him and then scrambled a couple eggs for breakfast. Once her belly was full she cleaned up her kitchen. She didn't have any plans for today besides housework and vegging with a good book, maybe watching some old movies on TV, one of her favorite past times.

Tabby walked into her living room, lit her candles and curled up on the couch. Her mind drifted toward memories of last night. She really had a good time. It was like the old Friday's before she and Nico started fighting. Actually it was better. Her group of close friends was growing and she thanked her lucky stars to be a part of it. It felt good to have people close to her that she cared about, that cared about her in return.

She'd always had her girls. Bri and Kaylee meant more to her than any two people in her life. Then she gained Luciano, a man that was like a brother in law to her. Now Nico, someone she could talk with, joke with and be herself around.

Charming jumped onto her lap. Tabby stroked her head listening to her cat purr in response. Boredom made her jumpy. She planned on staying home today but her original plan felt mundane. She wanted to do something, be around her friends.

Picking up the phone she tried Kaylee first but found out they had a cake testing appointment today. She dialed Bri next.

"Hello."

"Hey girl, what's up?" Tabby asked.

"I'm visiting with Mama Love. She was mugged last night." She could hear the concern in her friend's voice. Mama Love owned the house Bri lived in. It was a large, Victorian home that the older woman had turned into apartments. She was a wild lady for her age. In her younger years she'd been a hippie and her house had been a commune. Sometimes it seemed like Mama Love still thought it was the sixties and she was forty years younger. "Is she okay?"

"Yeah, she's okay. Just being stubborn as always. She wants to walk to her yoga class but I'm not letting her out by herself. What's up with you?"

Well that meant Bri wouldn't be leaving the house. She could always go there but had a feeling she'd be just as bored sitting around Bri's house as she was at her own. "Nothing. Just bored. You go ahead and take care of Mama Love. I'll talk to you later." Bri said goodbye and they ended the call.

Tabby stood up, Charming jumping from her lap as she went. After showering and dressing for the day she headed back to her phone. Maybe she'd see if Nico had any plans for the day. If he did then she'd head into the office and see if she could get any work done.

Flipping through caller ID she found his phone number and hit talk. The phone dialed his number and a tired sounding Nico picked up on the fourth ring.

"Hello," he grumbled.

Oops. She glanced at the clock and it was 9:30 AM. "Sorry,

Unexpected Mr. Right 49

I didn't think you'd still be sleeping. I'll let you go."

"It's cool. I'm up now." His voice sounded thicker, rougher…sexier. Kind of hot. Not that she would tell him that. It crossed the line on their friendship guidelines.

"Do you have any plans for today?"

"Not really. I'm going to order Luciano and Kaylee's wedding gift. That's all I really had planned."

She didn't know why but that surprised her. It shouldn't, Luciano was his cousin and they were close but their wedding was still a while off. She hadn't even decided what she was getting them yet. "Mind if I tag along? I'm itching to get out of the house and both Kay and Bri are busy."

"I see how you are. I'm you're last resort, huh?"

"Aw, does poor little Nico have his feelings hurt? Bet you haven't come across a woman who doesn't have you on the brain 24/7."

"You think about me, Tabby. Admit it."

"And feed into your ego? I don't think so."

"You just did, Slugger."

Damn. She didn't think about that when she spoke. "Well you think about me too, don't you? What's the big deal?"

"The big deal is I'm not afraid to admit it. You are."

He had her again. He was too good for his own good. Or her good actually. "So do you want company today or what?" Better to change the subject before she got herself into any more trouble. He had a way of getting her to say things she knew she shouldn't, to admit to feelings she didn't want to admit.

To her surprise Nico sat quiet for a few moments before responding to her. From her experience with him, he usually jumped at an opportunity when he found something that really interested him. His delay spoke volumes. So this was it. He'd realized just a friendship would be too much work. Trying to avoid an awkward moment she said, "Actually, never mind. I'm thinking I might just hang here today." Without much affect she tried to push her disappointment aside. She wanted to spend some more time with him. To gain that friendship they'd agreed upon.

She heard him exhale a heavy breath before he said, "Wait. I'm not letting you off that easy. I'll be there in an hour." He hung up the phone.

Nico almost told her no. Almost. He thought about what Luciano said to him the night before. *"Tabby's looking for that happily ever after and if you're not, I'm afraid she'll get hurt."* The idea of hurting her sat like a heavy weight on his chest. If he ever did want to settle down, it would be with a woman like her. But he wouldn't. Not for a long, long time at least. And she knew that. Hell she knew it better than he did. She reminded him every chance she had. He didn't have to worry about her forgetting it. Because of that, he knew she wouldn't get hurt. Not only would he not let her, she wouldn't either.

So he knew he could say yes like his body begged him to do. Knew he could indulge in this new friendship they were forming. He just hoped like hell he wasn't making a mistake. He'd never forgive himself if he hurt her.

Tabby sat next to Nico in a cab as they headed downtown. She wasn't sure exactly where they were going but it didn't really matter. She just enjoyed getting out of the house and spending time with him. "Do you already know what you're getting them?" she asked.

"Yep." Nico pulled a picture of Kaylee and Luciano out of his pocket. They were hugging one another, holding each other. "I wanted to do something special for them." He handed her the picture. "I'm getting this put on a plaque. Underneath the picture it will say, *Il vero amore e senza rimpianti.*"

His words flowed through her ears and landed with a smack in her chest. They were musical. "That's beautiful. What does it mean?"

Unexpected Mr. Right   **51**

"The real love is without regrets."

She looked at him utterly amazed by his words. He'd put a lot of thought into this. Nico had a romantic side. She couldn't have been more surprised by the knowledge. Apparently she wore her shock on her face. "What?" he asked. "Don't look at me like that. You should have seen what I really wanted to do. Photoshop a leash around Luciano, maybe throw a ball and chain in there. Then I decided I should go with the whole fairytale thing and not be so realistic."

At first Tabby could do nothing but stare at him in utter shock. She didn't know if his words were serious or meant as a joke. In reality, she thought probably a mixture of each. Thank God they were just hanging out as friends. When he winked at her she realized that he'd really been joking. Unable to hold back she playfully punched him in the arm.

Nico rubbed it. "Handicap me why don't you? I might not be able to use this arm for the rest of the day, you know? And you wonder why I call you Slugger." The last part he whispered.

Yeah right. She knew better than to think that punch hurt him. "And the Oscar goes to…"

"I see how you are. Give me a hard time for trying not to bruise your ego. I think you think you have an arm on you. Sure like to use it a lot."

Tabby gave him the evil eye and Nico held up his hands as if in surrender.

"Hey, don't hit me again. I'm just teasing you."

"Mr. Serious make a joke? No way." They both started to laugh. A few seconds later when silence commenced in the car she said, "Seriously. I think your gift is very sweet, Nico. I'm surprised."

"You give me no credit, Tab. Just because I have no plan of tying myself down to one woman for the rest of my life doesn't mean I don't know what love is."

"You don't want that for yourself?" she couldn't help but ask.

"Not right now. I have everything I need in my life. I'm truly happy and I enjoy my freedom. I don't know if I'll ever want to give that up."

"Loving someone shouldn't mean giving something up, Nico. If it does, what you get in return is so much more that it makes the sacrifice worth it." She felt that deep to the marrow of her bones.

"You're right. That's my point. I don't see how I could be any happier than I am now. If and I mean a big if I ever were to decide to settle down with a woman she'd have to be special enough to make me want to do it with no regrets. She'd have to add that much joy to my life. I don't know if I ever see that happening. Everyone is built differently, Tabby."

They were definitely built differently. That was the main difference between them. While he thrived on the single life, she yearned for something more, something bigger. *"We're built differently,"* she clarified.

"We make great friends though, Slugger."

She smiled agreeing with him. "That we do."

They went to a little engraving gift shop and ordered Nico's wedding gift. Noticing a coffee shop a couple doors down they headed over, ordered drinks and sat at the outside tables.

"Doesn't Bri have a coffee shop?" he asked.

"Yeah but can you imagine her reaction if we showed up together?"

"Oh yeah. I forgot you're hiding me," he said with a wink.

God that sounded so bad when he said it. "I'm not hiding you. I just don't want them to get the wrong idea."

"They'd harass you for spending time with a heathen like myself?"

Not really. It's not Nico they thought a heathen but Tabby who they thought couldn't take care of herself. How did she explain it to him without making herself look foolish? "It isn't you they won't trust, it's me. They'll be scared I'll fall for you." She sipped her latte. "They know my dreams better than anyone else. They're scared that I pick the wrong people to try and accomplish those dreams with." The words made her sound so needy. She hated it. She really didn't need a man, she wanted one. In her mind there was a big difference.

Nico's eyes diverted away from hers looking at the brown umbrella over their small, round table. Cars raced by, horns blared, people walked the streets. She watched him look everywhere except at her. "You won't, will you?" he finally asked. "Fall for me I mean. You want a future and I want a good time. Our ideas of a relationship are completely different. I don't want our friendship to give you false hopes."

In the beginning she fear that herself. That was part of the reason she avoided him, denied him for so long. Now, she really just enjoyed spending time with him. Enjoyed having him as a friend. And she wanted to know that she could relax a little bit, have some fun without worrying if this man happened to be *the one*. With Nico, she didn't have that stress. She knew from the start they weren't meant for one another.

"Relax, Romeo. You have nothing to worry about. I know where you and I stand."

He looked relieved as sexy a little smile stretched across his face. "Good. Now how about we run to the store and pick up a few things. I'm going to give you your first cooking lesson."

Tabby beamed. She couldn't wait.

"Where are we headed?" she asked as they climbed back into a cab a little while later.

"Valentino's to pick up a few groceries." They sat quietly as the driver brought them to the store. He couldn't help but think about the conversation at the coffee shop. When she again brought up the fact that she didn't want her friends to know about their friendship he'd been angry, but then he realized she was right. Just like Luciano, they'd all make their assumptions, getting on his back for doing something that he didn't plan to do. He wouldn't hurt her, couldn't hurt her. She knew the score.

She wanted it this way just as much as he did. *Maybe more*, he thought. Nico fidgeted in his seat trying to ignore the gnawing irritation in his gut. She didn't want the whole friend's thing more than him. Couldn't. He never wanted more than friends and this wasn't any different.

A few minutes later they pulled in front of Valentino's. Nico asked the driver to wait before opening the door for them to get out. "This is your first lesson," he said as they walked into the store. "Always buy your ingredients for Italian food at an Italian market."

She didn't look too convinced when she asked, "Things are so different here than at a regular store?"

"Oh yeah." He smiled. With that she shrugged and turned to scope out the isles with him.

"So what are we making?" She asked.

"I was thinking something simple for your first lesson. Something everyone likes."

"And that is?" she prompted.

"Pizza."

"I have the number for Domino's on my fridge at home."

He liked this light-hearted, playful side of her but still to compare homemade to take out was blasphemy. "I'm going to pretend you didn't say that, Slugger."

"Oh you take your pizza making very seriously." She rubbed her hands together as if plotting something. "Now I know how to get to you. I've heard the saying the way to a man's heart is through his stomach but with you it's a way to put a dent in you ego."

"Takes more than that to dent steel." Nico knew the line skated the edge of corny but that made it all the more fun. He added a wink and a smile to keep her on the edge. Every time he did that, heat spread to her cheeks. He liked to see that curious, sexy blush on her face.

"Okay I'm not going to justify that comment with a reply. Can we just get what we need before I'm unable to hold in my laughter and make a scene in this store?"

Nico let her off the hook by grabbing her hand to lead her through the store getting freshly grated mozzarella, parmigiano, and romano, fresh basil, tomatoes, and other seasonings. They went to the meat department and he had Italian sausage ground for them. "Do you have a pizza pan?"

"Puhleez. I told you, I do Dominos."

Nico grabbed one then told her, "This is for you. I expect you to use it after today."

"I will," she promised then assured him she had everything else they needed for dinner. Nico paid and they were on their way. He couldn't wait to show her what he could do in the kitchen. Feeding her at Luciano's and actually showing her the craft he loved were two totally different things. Sharing his love of cooking made him happy. A good meal could heal a lot of things. He just hoped she liked it. Thinking of Tabby working with him in the kitchen was a damn sexy thing. Kitchen tables were good for more than just eating on.

When they arrived at her apartment, Charming greeted them at the door. He immediately purred and rubbed his head against Nico's leg.

"I didn't know you had a cat. She must have been hiding the other day."

"Charming isn't a big people person. He usually hides out when people are over. I'm surprised he's giving you love right now. Do you like cats?"

"I love cats, Slugger." He kneeled down on her white carpet stroking Charming. "I've always been a *kitty cat* kind of man."

She had a feeling they weren't talking about the feline variety anymore. Leave it to Nico to find a way to make everything sexual. "Well, this one's a boy. He doesn't swing that way and I didn't think you did either."

He laughed heartily, stood up and walked into her kitchen. Tabby found herself following. "I don't. I go for tall, leggy, smooth, coco skinned, beauties who lately, have a habit of shooting me down."

"Maybe you're losing your touch?" *Yeah right.*

"It's not the ninth inning yet, Slugger. I still have time."

"You're right. The games over."

"Overtime?"

"Friends," she reminded him.

"With benefits?"

"You're not that lucky, big guy. Try again."

"I'm starting to see that. Just wanted to make sure you didn't suddenly realize a night of sweaty, no-strings-attached sex was on the menu."

"Nope, I'm sticking to pizza."

Chapter Five

Nico started off by teaching her how to make the dough. To her surprise he didn't measure a thing. Really she shouldn't be shocked. Cooking was not only what he did for a living but obviously something he loved as well. He moved so comfortably in her kitchen. Even though he'd never cooked in it she could tell he was a professional in his natural habitat.

They put the dough aside to let it rise. He told her it would only take about three hours and while it did its thing they'd make the sauce. Nico poured chopped tomatoes in a bowl and added a little tomato paste.

Finally grabbed her measuring spoons he glanced up. "I'm going to show you how I like it. When you do it on your own you'll learn to mix, add, take away different seasonings to your taste. Right now we'll just use the Valenti special."

He measured out red wine, basil, garlic, salt, pepper and added them to the bowel with the tomatoes. Tabby watched, taking mental notes and hoping like hell she could remember.

"Wash your hands," he told her. Tabby did and met him back at the counter.

"I want you to mix it together."

Tabby reached to pull a mixing spoon when Nico's hand suddenly grabbed hers. She felt a tingle shoot up her arm.

"No. Mix it with your hands. You need to mash the tomatoes really good."

He pulled away. Ignoring the dancing flutter in her belly she eased her hands into the bowl and began to crush the tomatoes, mixing the seasonings together. As the juices sloshed through her fingers she looked over at Nico. He watched her intently, like he was a doctor teaching her how to perform a surgery rather than a chef teaching her how to make pizza. But the fact that he took his job serious and really, truly enjoyed what he did make her respect for him grow.

A second later he eased his hands in the bowl with hers. She hated to admit it but the tingle returned with his touch. This time it settled a little south of the twitter in her stomach.

"That's it. Really get in there and smash them," he told her.

Their hands touched, swam together in the mixture getting it just right. He didn't talk anymore, just watched her, their hands drenched in tomato sauce, pureeing what was in the bowl. "I think that's good enough," she said breaking the moment. His eyes diverted from hers to the bowl.

"Yeah, that was a little too much to tell you the truth." He raised his finger to her mouth. "Taste?"

She didn't know why she did it. Knew it was stupid but she opened her mouth and drew his finger inside. The sauce tasted good but the man tasted even better. Quickly she pushed his finger out with her tongue. "Tastes good." Tabby walked over to the sink and started to wash her hands. She wanted, no needed to get a little bit of space between them.

She ran her hands under the warm water watching the red sauce drip from her fingers and down the drain. Nico stood behind her at the counter still by the bowl. She didn't have to turn around to know he watched her. She *felt* his eyes on her back. They'd shared a weird moment just now. A moment that felt more than friendly.

"So we can kickback and let the dough rise. Then we'll finish."

The light tone in his voice made it easier for her to turn and look at him. "Alright." Tabby moved aside to let him wash his hands. She dried hers then passed to towel to him. After his hands were dried they both walked into her living room. Their

Unexpected Mr. Right

footsteps the only sound in the room. "When did you know you wanted to be a chef?" she asked sitting on the couch. The question popped into her head as she tried to think of something to say to break their silence. He joined her on the couch a second later.

"Cooking has always been a big part of my family. My mom cooked everyday. On Sundays we'd go to Luciano's or they'd come to our house and we always had homemade sauce. They were always really great times, good family and good food. Luciano and I would hang out, torture my little sisters, talk about girls, you know, the normal boy thing."

Her heart lurched with his words, with the look of happiness on his face when he talked about his family. God she wanted that, brothers and sisters, cousins, anyone she could be close with, who would love her and have time for her. People who would want to be with her, not leave her at home with a nanny while they ran around town.

Trying not to show her emotions she looked at Nico and waited for him to continue.

"One day Mama asked for my help. She wasn't feeling well, the girls were all gone, Dad was working in the backyard. It was an instantaneous connection for me. It's hard to explain but it felt right. I liked mixing different spices together, creating a meal from different ingredients. When the family sat down to eat it felt good that I was the one who'd fed them. I brought the family together to share a meal, to talk, just to be with each other." He ran a hand though his short hair, dark mussing it even worse. "Sounds crazy doesn't it, Slugger?"

She could hardly speak. Her words were trapped in her throat. They fought to bust free from their cage but were unable. Feeling tears begin to prick her eyes, Tabby cleared her throat when what she really wanted to do is clear her mind. "Not at all. I think you're very lucky, Nico." She didn't want him to know how much his words affected her. How something so simple sounded so perfect and loving.

"Why?"

"Your family. Their closeness, love for each other. It's

wonderful you could give them what they need and they could do the same for you." She obviously couldn't give her parents what they needed. She was the third wheel in a perfect, fairytale happy couple.

"They didn't need that from me but I liked giving it to them. All we really needed was each other." He had no idea how lonely, how worthless those words made her feel. She never had that. Before she met Bri and Kaylee no one ever needed her.

"You're lucky all the same," she tried to sound nonchalant. Nico grabbed her face, turning her to look him in the eyes. She did. They watched each other. It was like he tried to look into her soul, like he wanted to read her. She feared what he would say next. What he might ask her. No way could she tell him how she felt, why she wanted that unconditional love so much. She couldn't let him know she'd never had it.

To her surprise he said, "Why don't we turn on some music and get back in that kitchen. You're lesson isn't done yet, Slugger."

He'd just let her off the hook. She knew it to the bottom of her soul. Like she already didn't like him too much, her trust for him started to grow, even if just a little bit.

Nico held himself back from asking Tabby the questions he really wanted to. He almost failed but when he looked her in her eyes, saw a sadness he'd never witness in her before, he changed the subject. She didn't want to talk about it. Her eyes told him that loud and clear. He wanted the happiness back in her gaze. So he decided to do what he did best, lighten the mood, have fun, make her smile. Smiling women were his specialty.

Walking over to her stereo he said, "Tell me you have some good music choices in your collection. I'm not in the mood for sappy love songs."

She stood up and smiled. His heart beat wildly. Damn he

Unexpected Mr. Right

loved that gorgeous smile. He'd do anything to keep it on her face. He like making women happy, making them smile. Nico was a guaranteed good time. That's what he'd been told and it was okay with him. He liked being the one people turned to for fun. Nothing serious, just a good time.

For some reason it felt a little better than it usually did. He knew it had to be because she was becoming such a good friend, almost like family. Though her and Kaylee weren't blood, they were family and in a short time Kaylee would be related to him so it would make sense his feeling extended toward Tabby.

Keep telling yourself that, man.

"Yeah, put on some Marley," she told him.

Good choice. He liked Bob Marley. Nico found the CD and put it in her player. As the Reggae beat started to drift from the speakers he grabbed for her hand.

"Show me some of your moves, Slugger." To his surprise, he didn't have to ask twice. Tabby started to sway her hips to the upbeat tempo.

He stood still watching her. Damn the woman was beautiful. And she knew how to move her body. A hard-on started in his pants. He wanted her now even more than before. There was something about her he couldn't shake. The more he got to know her the more his attraction for her grew. If only she'd realize how much fun they could have together. Inside the bedroom. The look on her face told him she knew the kind of fun they had outside.

As she continued to move, her body rocking back and forth sensually a thought struck him. He'd never be satisfied, never ease the ache in his body for her until he had her. He'd kind of started thinking the friendship thing would be enough. But it wouldn't. *Well, hell.* That didn't bode very well for him. She was determined not to give into his fiendish ways. She wanted forever with someone and that was the furthest thing from his mind. Wasn't it?

"Don't leave me hanging, Nico. It's no fun dancing by myself." Her words jerked him from his thoughts.

Oh yeah he'd like to show her his moves alright. The shitty part was the moves he wanted to share with her weren't the ones she spoke about. What the hell? When did he turn into the man who couldn't get the woman he wanted? Tabby was different than any woman he'd ever known. Not that he was a conceited guy but he'd never been so blatantly turned down before. No matter what he did he couldn't change her mind.

Nico pulled her against himself and began to move with her. Their bodies moved together with the fast beat of the music. She was soft, feminine. He put his hands on her thin waist feeling each movement of her body. Damn he wanted to explore her. As his hands moved he felt the rise of her ass below his finger. Inhaling a deep breath her lavender scent invaded his senses. Between that and the feel of her body he couldn't help but harden even more. He strained behind his confining jeans.

He spun her away from him so she wouldn't notice. She obviously thought it was part of the dance because she spun away still moving to the beat. Her hands began to mold to her own body as she danced sensually. He felt a jerk in his pants so strong he wasn't able to hold back. Nico reached for her determined so show her what their bodies could do *together*.

Clasping her hand he pulled her toward him right when Charming ran between them. Tabby tripped while trying not to hurt her cat and almost fell but he held her steady. Her head tilted back and she laughed joyfully.

"I needed that," she said after her laughter stopped. "Thanks, Nico."

Moment broken. Just like that. "I aim to please, Slugger." Please or not, he couldn't take anymore dancing. Not with her. "Come on, let's go finish dinner."

Tabby did everything Nico told her. She liked seeing him in his element. He explained all the steps to her as they did them and before she knew it her kitchen was filled with the

Unexpected Mr. Right   **63**

succulent smells of Italian herbs and they were pulling a delicious looking pizza from the oven.

"Mm. I can't wait to eat some of that," she said licking her lips.

"Since you're the chef, you get the first piece."

"Are you sure you're not saying that because you're scared I poisoned you or something?" she kidded.

He winked. "Naw, I kept an eye on you just to make sure."

Tabby grabbed two plates while Nico cut the pizza. He put a couple slices on each plate and walked them over to her table. She brought wine over for each of them. "I'm not waiting," she picked up a piece and took a bite. The cheese stretched so she broke it off with her fingers and set her slice down. It was delicious. The cheeses blended perfectly, the sauce was just right. "I'm so making this more often. You'll have to write down everything we did so I'm sure to get it right."

"I'll write it down for you but I think you could do it on your own. You're a natural."

"Thanks. I had a really good time doing it too." This had been one of the best days she'd had in a very long time. Nico made her happy, made her smile. He might not be Mr. Right material since he never wanted to settle down but he made a great friend. He kept her mind off her heartbreaks of the past.

"Want to watch a movie after we eat?" she asked after swallowing her second bite.

"Sure."

"I'm warning you now, I may have to pick a sappy love movie." She felt different around him. Light, if that made any sense. Like she didn't have to worry about being perfect, about finding that perfect man and making the perfect wife. That's the best word she could use to describe her parents. Absolutely perfect in every way. Dad the perfect man, Mom the perfect wife and she'd always been the imperfect daughter. But they'd really and truly loved each other. No one had ever loved her the way they loved one another. *Don't think about that right now.*

"You like torturing me don't you? In any way you can."

"Well it's fun and you have to admit you're an easy mark," she teased him.

"For you I am." He held eye contact with her. Tabby broke the connection.

"Please. I'm no different than any other woman to you."

"Did you know I haven't kissed or even gone out with another woman since our lip lock in Luciano's office?"

Her heart dropped and for a minute forgot to beat. Wow, they shared that kiss before Luciano and Kaylee were engaged. Hell it was before they admitted their feelings for each other. For a compulsive dater that amount of time must feel like an eternity.

Nico took a bite of his pizza but continued to watch her.

"Okay let me rephrase that, the only reason I'm different is because I continue to turn you down. I think that's why you proposed this friendship thing too. The only reason I intrigue you is because I can say no."

"The reason doesn't matter."

To her it did. They were such different creatures. She wanted to find the one, and settle down. Even if right now she wasn't going there, the thought still lingered in the back of her mind like an annoying fly that wouldn't go away. A guy like him enjoyed his freedom too much. If he ever did consider settling down it probably wouldn't last. She'd failed at love long enough to know the score. "It does to me."

He took a drink. "I know it does. For some reason I just wanted you to know, that's all."

Tabby's fingers held the stem of her wine glass, twisting the crystal, making the deep burgundy liquid slosh around in the glass. *For some reason I just wanted you to know, that's all*. Her mind echoed what Nico said. Maybe if she replayed the words she could figure out what he meant. Of all things she expected him to say she hadn't been ready for his little disclosure. A jittery excitement surged through her body even though she knew it shouldn't. What did she care if he'd kissed another woman since their short lip lock in Luciano's office?

But the fact was she did care. Selfishly, she liked the fact that

Unexpected Mr. Right   65

for whatever reason Nico kept his distance from women lately. *All women but me.* Before she had the chance to read anything into his words Tabby stood up from the table but she couldn't keep her eyes off him. He was such a sexy man and the woman in her couldn't help but desire him. Her feet stuck to the ground as if rooted there. Even when he stood up, took the glass from her hand, pushed the plates out of the way she couldn't move.

The look in his eyes, want, need, desire spelled out what he planned to do next. There wasn't a damn thing she could do about it, well actually there wasn't a damn thing she *wanted* to do about it. Not right now. Tabby let him turn her, his body pushed hers until the backs of her legs hit the table. Nico grabbed her, lifted her until she sat on her kitchen table and then he kissed her. A bone melting, heart racing, toe curling kiss.

At this moment she wanted nothing more than this sexy man and the things he did to her body. Sexual feelings no man ever stirred in her before. He made her *want* him, need his hand on her more than she needed her next breath. He oozed blatant sexuality from every pore in his body. He made her forget herself. When had her legs opened so he could stand inside of them? When had her hands wrapped around his neck?

Nico took her places she'd never been before, with just a kiss. He made her body burn, the apex of her thighs throb, her nipples tighten. He kissed her deeply, thoroughly, like a starving animal devouring his prey. She felt his urgent need as strongly as it built inside her own body. This was too good. He was too good. *Friends. You're supposed to just be friends.*

Right as the thought processed in her brain he left her mouth and started kissing his way down her neck.

"I told you there is more than one thing to do on a kitchen table," he whispered next to her ear. His words along with her thoughts seconds before gave her the momentum, *or stupidity*, she needed to pull away. As much as her body hated to, she knew she needed to stop this before they went any further.

"I'm sorry." Her voice came out much weaker than she wanted it to. "I can't do this, Nico. It's friends or nothing."

His eyes closed for a few seconds. When they opened he put his hands on her shoulders. "No reason to be sorry, Slugger. You told me the score from the get go."

She silently thanked God for his understanding. He wasn't used to women like her. Women who could easily indulge in what their bodies wanted. "We still doing a movie?"

"Of course. You can't get rid of me that easily."

Nico watched the credits roll across a black screen. He hadn't watched most of the movie. About a quarter of the way through, Tabby had fallen asleep, curled up on the other end of the sofa. He watched her instead, the rise and fall of her chest, the beaded nipples showing through her shirt. The why of it was what he couldn't understand. Whatever the hell it was, he was getting sick of it. The compulsion to tell her he wasn't dating, hadn't dated came from nowhere. It was a big mistake.

Giving her something to look at the wrong way, something that might make her think he felt something different than he did wasn't his smartest move. She had his whole game screwed up. He was doing things he never did, saying things he never did, feeling things he never did. But he couldn't put his finger on what it was. He knew nothing changed for him, he wasn't thinking about the whole white picket fence and two point five kids but he did want her more than ever.

And then there was the kiss. He knew she'd stop him but he'd been unable to stop himself. She cast some kind of spell on him that made him fall prey to stupid, compulsive activities that would only make him hornier, and her pull farther away. Still he continued to do it, continued to put himself out there to have a woman who didn't want him. But he couldn't get enough of her. Usually he would be tired of a woman by now, ready to move on.

Maybe he wasn't ready to move on because they hadn't

really gone anywhere yet. He hadn't had her yet. Hadn't sunk deep into the wetness of her body. Tabby moaned a soft sound that made him instantly hard. Damn. He'd always loved sex but he'd never had a constant hard-on around a woman before. He knew with her, the sex would go above and beyond any that he'd had before. That's what kept him going, kept him trying. That and the fact that he plain liked her. Everything about her.

Before he did something he'd regret, like waking her up and again kissing her senseless, Nico stood up and grabbed a blanket off the back of the couch. Softly, making sure not to wake her, he laid the blanket over her and turned off the TV. He slipped into her kitchen. Her cat sat by an empty food bowl. He looked in her cabinets until he found the food, poured some in the bowl and then grabbed a piece of paper and pen that sat next to her phone.

Slugger,
Remind me not to watch a movie with you again. You fell asleep within fifteen minutes. Didn't have the heart to wake you. Hope you slept well. If you want anymore cooking lessons (or anything else for that matter) you know who to call.
Nico
P.S. Charming was hungry so I fed him for you.

Nico put the note on the coffee table and slipped out the door making sure to lock it behind him.

Tabby rolled over and almost fell off the couch. She'd been so exhausted she didn't realize she'd fallen asleep in the middle of their movie last night. Stretching she looked down and noticed her blanket on top of her. Nico must have done it. *How sweet.* She sat up and happened to glance down at a piece of paper on the table. A note from Nico. Picking it up she read his words. Her heart skipped a beat.

Chill out girl. All the man did was feed your cat. Don't start romanticizing him. She couldn't let herself do that. She'd start thinking little things were cute and the next thing she'd know she'd fall for him and he'd lose interest and move on to his next conquest. Tabby stood up and folded the blanket putting it back on her couch. It really was sweet of him to cover her and feed Charming. But sweet in a friendly way not a romantic way. She'd have to thank him the next time they saw each other.

Walking into her bathroom, Tabby turned on the bath. She lit her lavender candles, put her bath salts into the tub and began to strip. A few minutes later she lowered herself into the water. It felt divine. Baths were her mode of relaxation. Nothing put her body at ease like a hot bath. Especially in her deep, jetted tub.

Leaning back in the tub she let the water take her to another place. Her thoughts were free to flow as she relaxed and damned if they didn't head straight to a very sexy Italian man who taught her to cook, covered her, and fed her cat. Every time she turned around he showed her a different side of him. Each one she liked more and more.

This surprised her, scared her, and excited her all at the same time. He wasn't like anyone she'd ever known which made him dangerous to the heart that she tried to guard. Being friends with him, and seeing this new side of Nico wasn't what she thought it would be. Nico was so much more in a way she wouldn't have imagined. He read her like he knew more about her than she did herself.

Last night's impromptu cooking lesson had been just what she needed. Well that and the dancing and talking. *And the kissing*. Time to switch topics. Cooking was much safer than kissing. Maybe next time she'd have him show her how to make an Italian dessert. Her stomach growled in response. She enjoyed this new friendship more than she thought she would. No matter his stance on relationships, Nico was a good guy. Just not the guy for her. For the first time she was a little sad by the acknowledgment.

Tabby let her water drain and toweled dry. After dressing she picked up the phone to call Bri. She wanted to hang with

Unexpected Mr. Right

her girls today. The guilt over keeping a secret from them bothered her. "Hey girl," she said after Bri picked up.

"What's up?"

"Want to get together today?"

"Sure," Bri replied. "I just got off the phone with Kaylee and she's busy with her Italian Stud but we can hang. I need to head down to Coffee Hut and check on the new girl but other than that I'm free."

"I'll meet you there. I want one of those blueberry bagels. They're to die for."

"I know I'm good. You don't have to tell me," she said with a laugh.

"You're so crazy, Bri. I'm going to head out and catch a cab right now. I'll see ya soon.

"Bye, girl."

"Later."

Tabby arrived at Coffee Hut about forty minutes later. She stepped into the small coffee house to find Bri behind the counter talking to a woman who looked to be about ten years older than them. She was so proud of her friend for starting her business. Her space rent was outrageous but it was her dream so she followed it. Luckily she paid really low apartment rent so the two evened out. Mama Love took a liking to her. Basically she just liked having Bri around. Since she didn't really need the money it worked out perfect for both of them. All her boarders were more for her company than anything.

"What do you want, Tab?" Bri asked.

"Caramel latte and a blueberry bagel." Tabby sat down on one of the two love seats in the shop. Neither matched but they were comfortable. Besides the couches there were six, small round, black tables with two chairs at each. Coffee Hut was small, cozy. The aroma of coffee permeated the air adding to the relaxed atmosphere.

Out of no where Tabby thought about Nico. She wondered if he ever wanted a place of his own or if Luciano's was his dream. Their family was so close she liked the idea of the two cousins sharing their dream together. Weird how she thought of him for no reason. Seem lately he popped into her head at the strangest times.

"What has you so lost in thought, girl?" Bri asked as she sat down and handed Tabby her drink and plate. Tabby leaned over and set her latte on a side table in between the two couches.

"Nothing important. How's business going?"

"Pretty good. I'm still trying to get things off the ground. I'm so lucky to have Mama Love. She's the one who referred Andrea to me. She's a stay at home mom who was looking for part-time work here and there just to get out of the house. She's willing to work for minimum wage and sometimes she works for me in exchange for babysitting. Otherwise I'm not sure I could afford to have anyone working for me."

Tabby had so much respect for her friend. She was strong, independent, and didn't take shit from anyone. She didn't need anyone but loved to be around people all the same, chatting, joking, and just having a good time. Actually, she reminded her of a female version of Nico. *Why does everything make me think of him?* "You know if you need help I'm always here for you. I could pick up some weekend hours anytime."

No matter what, she, Bri and Kaylee were always there for each other. They were sisters in every meaning of the word. "Thanks, girl, but I'm doing okay for now. I'll let you know if things change."

Tabby took a bite of her bagel and then swallowed a sip of her latte.

"Want to head back to my place with me? We can hang for a while." Brianna asked her after she finished her snack.

"Sounds like fun to me." A few minutes later they were out on the street hailing a cab back to Bri's house.

After visiting for a while at Bri's, her pug, Stud Muffin, began to prance in front of the door letting them know it was time for him to go out. Tabby liked going for walks so she decided to join them. She kicked a small rock across the sidewalk making Stud Muffin go crazy barking and jumping. Only Bri would name her dog Stud Muffin. According to her,

Unexpected Mr. Right   *71*

the dog was the only Stud she would ever keep in her life permanently.

She wouldn't be surprised if that was true. Bri never kept a man in her life. But she seemed to be happy and that's all that mattered. She couldn't help but hope someday Bri would settle though. For some reason, she thought her friend really wanted to but for some reason she just didn't.

"So how did the make-up between you and Nico happen?" her friend asked surprising her with the question from out of the blue.

Tabby chose her words carefully. She really didn't want to lie to her friend. "I realized I'd been a bitch to him. He apologized numerous times and I decided it was time to forgive him."

A curious glimmer sparked in Bri's eyes. "Well I'm glad for that. Is he still hounding you to go out with him?"

"You know, Nic. I don't think he could stop flirting if he had to. I know it comes from inside his pants rather than his heart so we're all good."

"Nic, huh? I don't remember you calling him that before."

Oops. "Nic, Nico. Whatever, it's the same thing to me."

Bri looked at her and smiled just as they approached her house. "Watch your heart, Tab. Nico's not the marrying type." Her words halted when she turned to face her house. A tall, very built man with dark blond hair stood at the side of the house trying to jimmy a window open. Before Tabby could stop her Bri set out running towards the burglar. Stud Muffin yapped right on her heels.

Brianna jumped on the man's back her arms flew around his neck. "You better leave Mama Love alone! How dare you try to break into her house. Isn't it enough that she was mugged?" Tabby watched in awe as the criminal staggered backwards obviously surprised a woman jumped onto his back. That made two of them. As he struggled to catch himself Stud Muffin barked and bared his teeth while trying to bite at his feet.

The man managed to catch himself without tripping over

Stud Muffin but barley. "This is my mother's house," he yelled, frustration evident on his face as he tried to shake Bri off his back.

Tabby ran forward to try and help her friend.

"Yeah right, Mister. I'm not falling for that," Bri replied clutching his hair and face to keep from falling. "Stay back, Tabby. Call the cops," she yelled.

"Yes, Tabby, whoever you are. Call the cops and while your at it tell them to bring a straight jacket for the lunatic on my back," the burglar yelled. Well maybe he wasn't a burglar if he wanted them to call the police. He almost tripped over Stud Muffin again. "And while you're at it can you call off the rat at my feet."

Tabby didn't know what to do. Call the cops or go help Bri. Something about the man in question told her he wasn't a burglar. He sounded too sophisticated, too pissed off at Bri for someone who should be running like hell if he really had been breaking and entering.

As if in slow motion Tabby watched the next few seconds unfold. Brianna yelling at their "burglar" and pulling backwards, Stud Muffin scurrying behind him trying to find a place to attack, the sophisticated burglar tripping over Stud Muffin and losing his balance. He fell hard to the ground taking Brianna with him. It was just the distraction he needed for Bri to let go. He flipped over, one leg on each side of Brianna, holding her arms above her head.

Burglar or not, Tabby wouldn't sit there while he held her friend. She lunged at him from behind and tried to pull him off of Brianna. "And you seemed like the level headed one," he said to her trying to shake her off. Her body rocked back and forth sharply.

"Leave my friend alone!" Stud Muffin rejoined the maylay now thinking it was a game and started licking Brianna's face as he pounced.

"She's the one who attacked me," he shook once more and Tabby lost her grip and fell beside him. Quickly he took one hand from Bri, still holding her wrists but one handed, and

Unexpected Mr. Right 73

wrapped his other arm around Tabby pulling her against him. "Now if you ladies would just calm down for a minute I'll explain to you why I was entering my mother's house through a window."

Chapter Six

Tabby relaxed in a hot bath for the second time in one day, her body aching from her tousle with a man they later found was named Jackson and he did in fact turn out to be Mama Love's son. Her police officer son who she expected but forgot to leave a key for so he was trying other avenues to get inside. Leave it to Bri to get her into that kind of mess.

As she let the warm water ease her achy muscles her phone rang. "Hello," she said into the receiver.

"Hey Slugger. How ya doing?"

Tabby let out a slight laugh. "You know, I really am Slugger today."

Concern laced his words when Nico asked, "What happened? Is everything okay?"

Did she really want to retell this story? She felt foolish. They must have looked like a couple lunatics wrestling around in the front yard. On the other hand it was pretty funny. Well it was pretty funny now. Not earlier.

Tabby started from Mama Love's mugging and then went into the whole story about finding Jackson trying to open her window, to Bri's attack, then her own toward the end. Nico sat quiet on the other end.

"It's okay, you can laugh. I still can't believe it happened," she told him.

"Naw, I won't laugh at you, Slugger. But you do know you

Unexpected Mr. Right   75

really aren't getting rid of the nickname now, don't you?"

"I kind of figured."

"Are you hurt?"

"My muscles are a little sore. Jackson tried to be careful, I think, but when he tried to shake me off him I think I pulled a muscle."

"Are you relaxing?"

"I'm in the bath as we speak."

He groaned into the phone. "Now there's a visual I'm going to imagine the rest of the night. I'm taking a break at work right now but I could come over after if you'd like. It would be late but I could give you a massage."

A vision of Nico rubbing his strong hands against her body popped into her mind. He'd work her muscles, giving her a deep tissue massage. *Yeah. So, not a good idea.* "Are you trying to seduce me, Mr. Valenti?"

"Just being a good friend. Unless that is, you've decided you're seducible."

A laugh escaped her lips. He always seemed to do that to her. Even on the phone she couldn't help but be happy around him. "Why would we want to ruin this wonderful friendship we're building?"

"We wouldn't have to ruin it. Friends make the best lovers," his tone went an octave lower, seductive.

"You just made that up." Tabby sank a little lower in the bath, a shiver racing up her spine. "Ouch. I have a serious kink in my neck." God the thought was so tempting. Her body wanted her to throw caution to the wind and let him come over give her the massage he promised.

"Close your eyes," he ordered.

"Why?"

"Just humor me, Slugger."

Okay, she had no idea what he had planned but what could hurt to humor him. They were on the phone so it wasn't like anything he said could really get to her, make her attraction for him come to live in ways she didn't want it to. "They're closed."

"I want you to relax and no matter what I say, don't argue with me. I'm going to tell you what I'd do to you if you'd let me."

Oh boy. She didn't know what he had in store for her but an eager ache started to form in the pit of her belly. That couldn't be a good sign.

"Grab a washcloth."

"I can't. You told me to close my eyes."

"Open your eyes and grab washcloth then close them again. And I told you not to argue with me." He sounded serious, authorative, a tone she wasn't used to hearing in his voice. Tabby did as he said, grabbing a rag and then leaning back in the tub.

"Now whatever goes on Tabby, is just between you and I. It doesn't change anything, we're still only friends, and we still aren't having sex so don't fight it, okay?"

"Okay," she heard the words come out of her mouth but couldn't believe she let herself utter them.

"Get the washcloth wet and rub it across your shoulder. Lightly, just kind of let it float across your skin. Softly."

She didn't reply but started to do what he said.

"Are you doing it?"

"Yes."

"Good but now I want you to pretend it's me. You're laying in the bath and I'm rubbing your shoulders." She started to call a halt but he silenced her with his words. "Don't run, Tab. I'm just trying to make you feel better. Your rules are still intact."

She could do this. She wanted to do this. She couldn't ever experience Nico first hand even though her body wanted to. It overstepped the bounds she put in place, it risked her heart with a man who she knew would never want to keep it. But this, this she could do.

"Roll the washcloth and put it behind your neck."

Tabby obeyed.

"Remember it's me. My hands are on your neck, Tabby. Do you feel the heat radiating off my skin?"

"Yes." Why the hell did her voice sound so breathless?

Unexpected Mr. Right 77

"You're hot too, Tabby. I feel your warmth as I'm rubbing your neck. My hands are kneading your sore muscles. Does it feel good?"

Goose bumps pebbled on her skin. "Yes," she replied. The word seemed to be all she could muster the strength to say.

"Good girl. I only want to make you feel better. You're skin is so soft, Tabby. I love the way it feels under my hands. I'm going to work my way up your neck, putting pressure with my thumbs and then I'll travel back down, okay?"

Y-E-S! She couldn't bring herself to reply out loud but knew Nico would understand. Damn he was good. Her body felt so loose, so at ease, so sensitive, like his hands were really caressing her skin. She felt her nipples begin to harden to peaks.

"I'm rubbing out all the tension in your neck, Tabby. Each time I feel a knot, I'll work it until it disappears leaving you feeling nothing but pleasure." She again didn't reply. "You doing okay there, Slugger?"

"Better than okay." Good God if this man made her feel this good "rubbing her shoulders" over the phone she couldn't fathom how she could ever handle being with him for real. It's a good thing she never planned to find out.

"Can I take this game a step farther, Tabby? Will you give me that much pleasure since I'll never be able to feel you beneath me?"

Her eyes popped open at his request.

"Close your eyes and relax, Tabitha. Don't think. Don't read too much into this. We're on the phone, playing a little game. Nothing changes. We're still just friends, no dating, no touching, no kissing, just this."

She almost asked him how he knew she'd opened her eyes but didn't. The answer scared her. Nico seemed to read her better than any man she'd ever known. It was probably all his experience, after all, women were his expertise. *Stop it. Don't go there. You're just friends so you won't get hurt.*

"I don't have much time left. If we're going to do this you need to let me get started."

"Yes," she pushed the single syllable word from her mouth. She couldn't manage anything more.

"Does your neck feel better? Can I move on?"

"Yes."

"My hands are working their way down your neck, Tabby. All the tension is gone as I rub my hands across your mocha skin. I'm at your shoulders. I'm not massaging anymore. Just tickling. Whispering my fingers across your body like a ghost. You can't see me but you can feel me can't you, Tabby?"

When did her name on his tongue start to sound so damn seductive? His voice hypnotized her. The ache in her belly headed south until it landed at the center of her thighs. "Yes, Nico. I can feel you."

"Say my name again. I never thought I'd get to hear you say it with that husky, turned-on, breathlessness that you have right now."

"Nico."

"Fucking beautiful. Just like you, Tabby. I think you deserve a reward for that. I'm going to touch your breast. Those pert little nipples are begging for me. They're eager for me. I can feel it as I roll them between my fingers. Do you like that?"

"Yes."

"Yes, who?"

"Yes, Nico."

"Don't deny me that, Tabby. I want to hear you say my name tonight. Can you do that?"

"Uh huh...Nico."

"You know what would make this even better for you? Move your hands to your own breasts. Pretend it's me, Baby. Roll your nipples and imagine it's my hands giving you pleasure."

Baby. He hadn't used any names like that for her since the incident when she slapped him. After that she was Slugger. Apparently not tonight. Her body warmed at the sound of the term of endearment.

"Are you doing it?" he asked.

Like they had a mind of their own, Tabby's hands moved to

her breasts, to her nipples. She squeezed, rolled and teased imagining it was Nico's hands on her. She needed this. They both did. The attraction they felt was mutual but she couldn't let it go any farther than what they shared right now.

"Tabby, Baby? You still with me?"

"I'm here. And I'm doing it. I'm touching...myself...like you said."

"Good girl. I wish I could be there to see you."

"You are here," she reminded him as she squeezed her own nipples.

He snickered. "You're right. I am and you feel so good. I'm going to put a little more pressure with my fingers. Damn you feel good in my hands but I think I want to taste you. I'm flicking your nipple with my tongue, next I'm going to draw it into the warmth of my mouth. Does that feel good?"

"Oh God, yes." Tabby felt him. All around her, sucking on her nipples with skill. "I'm so close, Nico." It surprised her that her bluntness didn't embarrass her.

"I'm switching to your right breast. My mouth is there sucking on you while my hand is on your left. We wouldn't want to leave anything out, would we? Damn you feel good, Baby. Let loose for me."

Tabby moaned her release into the phone. When she did she heard Luciano yelling Nico's name in the background. Damn.

"Shit," Nico hissed. "I have to go, baby."

Tabby almost couldn't speak her body lay so limp with satisfaction. But a thought popped into her head and she couldn't help but ask. "Wait," she called out.

"Yeah?" He sounded annoyed. Maybe that wasn't the right word. More like frustrated. Sexually frustrated.

"Do you still think I'm only vanilla with sprinkles?" She didn't know why she wanted to know but for some reason she did.

He let out a laugh sounding more like the man she started to know so well. "I think you just added a little chocolate sauce into the mix."

Jesus, he was hard as nails. Damn Luciano for coming in when he did. Better yet, for scheduling him to work tonight. If not he would be on his way to her house to finish what they started. Now that the moment ended, he wasn't sure he'd get it back. She'd start over-thinking it, worrying, stressing that he would hurt her.

But he wouldn't. Would he? All he wanted to do is spend more time with her, pleasure her, show her how good he could make her feel if she'd just loosen up and indulge in a good old fashion affair with him. She had time to look for Mr. Right later. They were young and free. Why not enjoy it?

Nico stirred the sauce that boiled on one of the stoves. She somehow gotten under his skin. That never happened before. It wasn't something he worked at, he just never met a woman like Tabby before. A woman he could laugh with, talk with, try and open her world a little bit. A woman who had desire in her eyes but was too afraid to indulge.

Except tonight. Tonight she'd pleasured herself, with him instructing her. Maybe there was a light at the end of the tunnel. But she'd have to make the next move. He didn't chase women. Well he hadn't until he met Tabby.

Tabby couldn't get her orgasm inspiring phone call out of her head. A couple days passed yet her cheeks still tinged with an embarrassed heat at the memory. Hell, maybe she should have gone to the doctor after her tussle with Jackson. Obviously the incident left her with a couple loose screws. Not much she could do about it now. Last she checked they didn't make pills to help crazy women who pleasure themselves on the phone with a man who was supposed to be *just a friend*.

Though the way she saw it they should.

She didn't do phone sex. Never had. The fact is, before Nico she was never a really sexual woman. Sure she'd had sex and enjoyed it enough but a man never gave her that zing with just one look the way Nico did. And you could sure bet no man

Unexpected Mr. Right   81

ever made her even think about tweaking her own nipples into orgasm while being coaxed over the phone with said man. "Oh God what have I done?"

Tabby leaned back in her office chair and let out a frustrated sigh. Now she had no idea how to act around him. He hadn't called her since *the incident* as she liked to call it. Was he giving her space? Had he decided to just move on? Would he expect something more from her now? She knew her actions sent out mixed signals. Not smart. This wasn't a game to her and she feared he would think it was. One minute she said one thing, the next she screamed in release while he sat listening on the other end of the line.

The scariest part is she feared she'd be even more attracted to him now. She always wanted him and if things were different, if she could indulge in an affair without risking her heart she'd have given in months earlier. After what they just shared she knew that idea to be even worse than she originally thought. If he could do what he did with just words she'd be in big trouble if she ever jumped into the sack with him.

The thing was even though she wanted nothing more than to forget *the incident* had never happened, she knew she couldn't. One look at him and she'd recall every passionate second of their phone call. Seeing him for the first time in front of Bri, Kaylee and Luciano on Friday night would be a huge mistake. They'd know something happened. Well lets rephrase that, she'd help them figure out something happened by turning into a shy, red-cheeked, ball of embarrassed energy right in front of them.

She'd be like Kaylee was around Luciano before they got together. "Shit, shit, shit." The only thing she could do is call him. Hope that they could talk this out and it would ease some of the awkwardness that would no doubt be between them. Grabbing her cell out of her purse she looked his name up in her phone book and hit send. Three rings later he answered.

"Hello."

"Hey…It's Tabby."

"I know who it is, Slugger but you are going to have to

speak up if you want me to hear this conversation. You're mumbling over there."

Was she mumbling? She hadn't noticed. Damn she felt silly. She had no idea what to say. He probably did stuff like this all the time. "Sorry. I just thought we should…um…talk about the other night."

"Why?" he asked.

Why? Why? Of all the dumb things to say. "Because I touched myself with you…over the phone!"

"Unfortunately, I didn't get to do any touching. Being at work and all. Maybe next time though." She could hear the smile in his voice.

"You know that isn't what I meant. We stepped over the lines of our friendship, Nico. Things weren't supposed to go…there."

"I don't live my life by a strict set of rules like you do. Who cares where things were supposed to go, that's where they went. I had a hell of a good time as I'm sure you did too but if you don't want that to change things it won't. Simple as that. We're still friends, I don't expect anything else out of you. End of story. Unless of course you want—"

"No." She cut him off. "I mean, I enjoyed the other night but we can't do it again. We just can't do it again." She envied how easy going he sounded about all this. No matter what she decided he was okay with that. She could never be like that. Not where sex and love were concerned.

"Okay, Slugger. No more hot-as-hell phone sex. What about cooking lessons? We still okay with those?"

To her surprise the word, "Yes," rolled out of her mouth without a second thought. She really wanted to spend more time with him. It might not be a good idea but she couldn't say no regardless.

"Great. Where are you?"

"Work."

"Give me the address. I'm picking you up in half an hour."

Unexpected Mr. Right   83

Tabby and Nico walked into building where Nico informed her they would be taking a cooking class. Why, she didn't know. The man was a freakin' chef yet they were taking a cooking class. His idea. Not hers.

They walked into the room, everyone already behind their station and the cooking teacher in the front of the room.

"Glad you could make it," the female teacher called out. "I'd heard I had two more for this evening. Do you want to tell us a little bit about yourselves before we get started?"

Nico spoke up before she had the chance. "My name is Luciano and this is my fiancée Kaylee. Neither of us know a thing about cooking so we decided to take a class before our upcoming wedding."

Tabby's head snapped to the left to look at him. She could feel her eye protruding from her head.

"Don't be shy Snooky," Nico pat her hand before turning toward the teacher and the rows of people who stood in front of them. "She's a little bit nervous because she can't cook."

The squeaky-voiced woman came toward them. "Now Kaylee, there's no reason to be shy. Everyone is here because they have trouble in the kitchen. We'll have you whipped into shape before that wedding date gets here."

She could practically hear Nico laughing even though no sound escaped his lips. She could feel his amusement seep through their touching hands. Well, two could play at that game.

"Luciano tried to show me how to cook macaroni and cheese one night, it's his favorite meal, you know, but he forgot to use a pot holder and burned his hand so bad we spent half the night in the emergency room. He's been so scared ever since I can hardly get him to step foot in our kitchen. It's like just seeing the stove gives him flashbacks."

How do you like that?

"Oh you poor dear. We'll cure you of your phobia today, you just wait and see. I'm going to pay extra attention to you throughout your lesson today. We couldn't want you to get injured again."

Tabby got him that time. He didn't expect her to come up with a story like that so quickly. Now he had an overbearing cooking teacher breathing down their backs the whole time they made their poached pears. He could work with this. Might as well get into character and enjoy the little game. They'd mixed the wine, cinnamon, nutmeg, water and a few other ingredients in the sauce pan. The pears needed to go in next. "Snooky, how about you take over? After all, you'll be the one cooking the most. While I'm working I'll need someone at home, barefoot and pregnant in the kitchen."

Nico tried to hold in his smile when every woman in the room looked at him like a chauvinist and the men looked at him with sympathy. When Tabby turned and shot him with her evil eye he knew he'd succeeded in what he really wanted to do, give her a hard time.

"Well Luci, since you're the one who has a phobia to get over I think you need this more than I do."

She added a little "Ha" with her eyes telling him she thought she'd just pulled one over on him.

"You weren't calling me Luci last night." He added a wink for good measure.

"Nico!" she screeched.

"Who's Nico," the chef asked?

"That's what I'd like to know." He fought to hold in his laugh.

She looked nervous. He could see the wheels turning in her head like she really wanted something creative to say. Lucky for her, their instructor saved her.

"Tonight is about the art of cooking. Let's focus on that. Luciano, why don't you add the pears. We want you to get over your fear of getting burned. Hop back on that horse by adding those pears and covering the pan with a lid."

This lady was a little crazy but a laugh all the same. He didn't want to ruin her class so he decided to get to cooking, of course still pretending he had no idea what to do. "Kaylee why don't we do it together?" It took Tabby a minute to realize he spoke to her.

She smiled up at him and it hit him right in the chest. She had a beautiful smile. It took him a minute to realize her smile was part of their act.

Tabby picked up two of the peeled pears and he grabbed the other. They placed them in the pan before he covered it.

"That's it. You two work very well together."

"Thanks," they both replied in unison. Yeah, he thought they worked well together too.

The pears simmered and apparently had to sit over night after that. While they did their thing the cooking instructor brought out already simmered pairs for them to start the second half of the recipe. Nico was such a character. She couldn't believe he threw out that whole Kaylee and Luciano scheme. She'd have never thought to do something like that but after he started the routine she realize how fun it really was.

Nico continued his spiel the whole time, grabbing huckleberries when they were instructed to grab vanilla beans, or questioning which spoon was the teaspoon compared to the table. She couldn't believe no one else caught on to their act. She felt herself smiling numerous times through their whole lesson. Despite the fact that he'd "messed" up the whole time their pears came out perfect by the end of the class. Apparently he couldn't screw up a recipe even when he tried.

When they walked out Tabby let out the pent up laughter that built inside her throughout their evening. "My cheeks hurt from smiling so much," she said once she stopped laughing enough to talk.

"I can't believe they actually believed I was had burn-a-phobia or something. That was a good line by the way."

"I learned from the best. You're starting to rub off on me."

"What can I say? I'm the friend who knows how to have a good time."

"Yes you are. I'm so glad we're becoming friends, Nico."

When she looked at him a wave of annoyance seem to wash over his eyes. As quickly as it drifted in, the look drifted back out. Who knows? Maybe she imagined the whole thing.

"Hey girl," Tabby heard Bri call as she stepped from the cab. They're arrived at the same time. To her surprise, Bri had a tall, man with her. He had smooth, dark skin and a shaved head.

"Hey you."

"This is Lance. He's a new boarder at Mama Love's. He's pretty new to the area so I told him he could hang with us tonight."

"Hi Lance. Nice to meet you." Tabby grabbed his outstretched hand and shook it. So much for girl's night out. Not that it really was that anymore anyway. With Nico and Luciano joining them the dynamics changed.

They turned and headed into the restaurant. Bri grabbed an extra chair and pulled it up for Lance. He sat between Brianna and herself. Kaylee, like always sat waiting for them. Brianna made her introductions and they all sat down chatting. To her surprise, Lance didn't pay much attention to the other ladies. He shot questions at Tabby left and right. What did she do for a living? What did she do for fun? How long had she lived here? And on and on. Every question, aimed at her. In some weird way she felt uncomfortable. Not that Lance did anything wrong but she felt like she was on a kind of date with him. And it didn't feel right. Like she was being unfaithful to someone which happened to be the stupidest thing she could ever feel.

"Have you ladies been friends long?" Lance asked Tabby another question.

"Yeah, since we were young."

"That's great. I left all my longtime friends back home. I'm looking forward to spending time with new people though."

Unexpected Mr. Right 87

He winked at her. *Huh, so Lance is a flirt.* He was an extremely good looking man but the way he looked at her annoyed her. Not at all like she felt when Nico looked at her. *What are you thinking about him for?*

"What made you move?" she asked trying to be polite.

"Bad breakup. I found out my fiancé cheated on me. Not the way I planned to start the rest of my life with someone so I called it off."

"I'm sorry but it sounds like you made the best choice. Better to find out now than later."

"True. I guess that means there's someone better out there for me," Lance said with a smile. "You have something on you," He reached his hand off and brushed her shoulder. "I'll get it for you."

Tabby glanced at the door to the kitchen right when Nico happened to stick his head out. He looked at her, at Lance who seemed to be taking an awful long time to brush something of her, then back at her again. A fire lit his eyes that she'd never seen before, making her heart pound in her chest. Then he disappeared back inside the kitchen.

Kaylee must have seen the look too because she bumped her leg under the table and gave her the, "What the hell was that?" kind of look. Tabby shrugged her shoulders playing it off as if she didn't know what she meant. Less than a minute later Nico stood behind her, plates full of pasta primavera in hand. He usually didn't come out this early. Luciano hadn't even made it to their table yet.

"Hello, Ladies. I didn't know someone else would be joining us tonight." His eyes locked with Lance's and the other mans eyes didn't turn away. Tension rolled off Nico so strongly she could feel it surrounding her. He set their plates down leaving an empty spot for Lance and pulled up a chair on the other side of Tabby.

"I have something special for dessert tonight." He looked around at everyone at the table but when his eyes landed on Tabby they stayed. "I think you're really going to like it, Sweetheart." Not Slugger. Sweetheart. What the hell was this all about?

Bri spoke up. She had a feeling she wasn't the only one who felt the tension at the table. "Hey, super chef. You got anything back there for Lance to eat tonight or does he just have to sit around and watch us?" Nico signaled a waiter over and asked for another plate.

"I didn't know you were dating anyone, Bri." He said.

"Please, I don't date. Lance is my new neighbor. He's looking to meet some people so I brought him with me."

"I was just getting to know Tabby a little bit while we waited," Lance said to Nico.

She actually felt Nico tense beside her. His jaw locked. Somehow she'd stepped into some weird parallel dimension where Nico acted like her jealous boyfriend which made no sense at all. Hell the man dated women like crazy. He didn't do boyfriend so she knew he sure didn't do jealous boyfriend.

"There are thousands of other women you could get to know in San Francisco. You should try one of them."

"Nico!" Anger coursed through her veins. She didn't really want to get to know Lance but she also didn't want Nico warning men away from her. He had no hold on her.

"What?" he looked surprised. "I'm being a nice guy. Just letting him know there's a wide variety of *other* women to choose from. Hell, I'll even introduce him."

Bri started to laugh. Kaylee looked concerned. Lance stared at Nico then finally nodded his head. Nico did the same like they just came to some agreement without words. At some point during the ordeal, Luciano had stepped up to the table and stood behind, Kaylee. "Nico, I need to see you in the kitchen. Now." He turned and walked away. Nico cursed and followed him.

He felt like a dick. That being said, having to do it over again, he would have done the same thing. No way would he chance the woman he'd lusted after for months on end

Unexpected Mr. Right   **89**

hooking up with another guy. No fucking way. Not Tabby. After what they shared on the phone the other night and after the way they clicked during their cooking class, he burned to have her even more. He would have her.

He'd been pissed when she called him her friend. He didn't know why, he'd said the same damn thing right before her but that was different. He didn't really want to only be friends with her. He did that to pacify her. The more she said it the more she proved to him that she really only wanted a friendship. That just didn't sit well with him. She wanted more. He knew it. The only question was how to make her see it.

"So what the hell made you act like that earlier, Nic?" Luciano said as they sat at one of the tables in the closed restaurant. "It's not like you to be so possessive over a woman. Especially one you aren't dating."

Shit. He knew it was coming. Knew Luciano would ask him. The truth was he didn't know how to reply. He didn't know what came over him earlier. Yeah, he wanted Tabby but she wasn't his. Hell, he didn't even want her to be his. Not for more than a few nights at least. His behavior earlier told a different story and he knew it.

When he looked out the kitchen doors and saw the guy talking with her, saw the look of hunger in his eyes he'd lost it. But he couldn't tell Luciano that. His cousin would take it to mean more than it did. He'd ask questions, questions Tabby wouldn't want him to answer. "I wasn't possessive. There's just something about that guy that rubbed me the wrong way. You said yourself that Tabby's looking to settle down. I just don't want her to get hurt."

Luciano blew out a breath with a humph. "Yeah, right. Try again."

Yeah, he knew Luciano wouldn't fall for that one. "You figured me out. I'm having a wild and crazy affair with Tabby. We've been going at it like rabbits for weeks. I knew once she had me, not other man would compare so I decided to put the bozo flirting with her out of his misery."

Nico tilted the cold bottle of beer back and downed it. Droplets of moisture dripped from the bottle down his fingertips. He didn't want to talk about this. Not with Luciano. Months before he pushed and pushed until Luciano realized he loved Kaylee. His cousin just might try and return the favor even though this was a completely different situation. Pulling a Nico and turning the situation into a joke would provide the distraction he needed.

Right on cue Luciano laughed. "Yeah, that's even more unbelievable than your first answer. You know there's only one Valenti man with that kind of skill with the ladies and it isn't you," he kidded.

"You wouldn't even know what to do with a woman if it wasn't for me. Come to think of it, I could probably set up my own little business like that Hitch guy. Teach 'em what the ladies really like. Hell, I could use you as my first satisfied client," Nico joked back even though his heart wasn't in it.

Talking about what women wanted wasn't enough. He wanted to show Tabby exactly what he could do. Show her how much more pleasure he had in store for her. The other night on the phone was just the beginning. Tabby wanted to fall in love, to settle down and even though she wasn't seeing anyone right now, he knew she would again. Seeing her talk to Lance reminded him of that.

Now was his chance. Their chance. The attraction between them forged a desire too strong to ignore. They would enjoy each other and then move on their way knowing they took advantage of the chance put in front of them.

Sounded good to him.

Now he just had to prove his point to her. Nico stood up and marched toward the door determination fueling him. He didn't care that it was midnight; he was going to see Tabby. Tonight.

"I guess we're done here?" Luciano called after him.

"We're done."

"I hope you know what you're doing, Nic."

Yeah, so did he.

A loud pounding jarred Tabby from a deep sleep. Her heart matched the beat. Something had to be wrong for someone to bang on her door at this time of night. Jumping from the bed she put her robe on over her silk negligee and raced toward the door. She peaked quickly through her peephole to see Nico pacing. Oh God, please let her friends be okay. Nico had no other reason to be at her house this late.

"What's wrong," the words squeaked out as she opened the door. She could hardly utter them. Fear almost blocked her speech.

Nico pushed his way into her apartment and closed the door with a bang. "Nothing's wrong, Slugger. If this night goes as planned everything will be right." And then he kissed her. His lips started out a slow sensual assault, lightly caressing her lips before drawing her lower one into his mouth. He was testing her. She could tell. Making sure she'd submit before he went any further.

He tasted lightly of beer but more of man. Hungry, eager man. She shouldn't do this. They wanted different things. Since she lost her virginity at eighteen she'd never been with a man that she didn't have deep feelings for and never planned to.

But the way his lips begged hers to join in she couldn't hold herself back. He was gentle but still owned her mouth, making it impossible not to kiss him back.

She realized then she did have feelings for him. Not the usual thoughts of love but friendship. A close camaraderie she'd never felt with another man. That eased her inner guilt. Not that she should feel guilt. There was nothing wrong with a single twenty eight year old woman sating her body with another equally single man. And that's exactly what her body wanted. To be sated. By Nico. Even if only this once.

If she didn't do this, she'd regret it. Her body's need for him was too strong. She'd never been an overly sexual woman, wanting more of an emotional connection than a physical one. With Nico it wasn't about love, it was about a physical need she had to explore. Then they would go back to the way they were and she'd know herself capable of holding her feelings in check when it came to intimacy.

Yeah, right.

Despite her thoughts Tabby wrapped her arms around him silently telling him she wanted this. That she wanted him.

"Thank God," he said against her mouth before he pinned her body tightly between the wall and himself and kissed her with a fierceness she'd never known.

Chapter Seven

Nico's mouth devoured hers. His kiss was hard, each sweep of tongue urgent. His body pressed against hers so tightly she didn't have room to move. Not that she wanted to. His long, hard erection rubbed against her as he pulled just far enough away to open her robe and push it half off her shoulders. "I love silk," he whispered against her mouth. He lifted the bottom of her negligee bunching it in his hand.

He moved his hand to touch her bare stomach. Her skin sizzled beneath his caress. "You're skin feels even better than any silk, Tabby," he said before thoroughly kissing her again. Her toes curled. She felt him on every inch of her body. He moved to cup her rear, his knee pushing her legs apart and settling between her thighs. "You're so wet. I can feel your heat against my leg. I knew you'd be so damn hot, Tabby."

"I'm usually not," she said breathlessly as his mouth kissed a trail down her neck. "It's like I'm on sensory overload," his knee ground against her femininity. She arched her neck back to give him better access. Nico took advantage and sucked her earlobe into his mouth. "I mean, it's not as if I've never had sex, or never had an orgasm, but this...damn your good," she couldn't help but say.

Nico moved back to her mouth and kissed her quiet. He pulled away and said, "You're rambling. We'll talk later. I need to get inside you. I have months of waiting to make up for."

Nico carried her to the bedroom. Setting her on her feet he didn't waste any time undressing her. He didn't want to give her the chance to change her mind. It would kill him. He pulled her robe completely off her shoulders and let it drop to the floor. Her nightgown followed seconds later. She stood in front of him in pink g-string panties and nothing else. "Damn woman, you're going to be the death of me."

He couldn't stop staring at her, soaking her in from her cute, red painted toenails to her frazzled hair. Delicious. Her skin a smooth, milk chocolate that smelled of lavender, begged to be touched. Her rounded breasts were pert, with hard pebbled nipples. Damn he wanted to taste them. And he would. First he needed the dark curls he saw beneath her pink panties uncovered. And he needed her to do it.

That would be her final concession. He had to know this is what she really wanted. That she desired him and wanted to proceed to the next level as much as he did. "Take off your panties." The urgent scratch in his voice didn't surprise him.

"I—"

"Do it, Tabby. I want to watch you ease that sexy scrap of cloth down those long legs. I need to know this is really what you want. No regrets." She looked apprehensive at first but the looked quickly turned into one of excitement, eagerness. Hooking her matching, red painted fingernails in the strap on the side of her panties she began to lower them.

Hell fucking yeah.

Her slender waist bent and she lowered the g-string down her legs. When she reached her feet she stepped out one foot at a time before straightening to stand beautifully naked in front of him. "*Cosi Caldo, cosi bella. Li Voglio.*" Nico eased her back on her plush bed. When her head rested on the pillows he started to kiss her. It was a short, demanding kiss before he moved down to her neck, kissing the hallow spot at the base of her throat.

"What...what does that mean?" she asked breathlessly, running her hands through his hair.

"So hot, so beautiful," he lowered his hand to cup her mound. "I want you."

"I want you too." The verbal admission almost sent him over the edge. He teetered there the whole time, but that, hearing those words almost did him in.

Nico rested between her thighs. "I don't know where to begin," he admitted. "I want to taste every inch of you, Tabby. How do I decide?"

She sighed, a sexy sigh as her eyes drifted closed as if waiting for him. Nico kissed her lips, "eeny," her left breast, "meeny," her right, "miney," then he eased down her body until his mouth was inches from her core. He lowered his head and licked. "Mo." Damn she tasted good, wet and sweet. This is where he needed to be. He had to start here.

Her body burned from the inside out. With each lick of his tongue the fires inside burned hotter and hotter, building closer to the explosion she knew was inevitable. Her skin sizzled under his touch. Nico ignited an inferno that she'd never experienced before.

She throbbed with need as his tongue swept between the folds of her sex, gently licking and probing. Her blankets knotted in her hands as her body writhed in pleasure. "Oh, God, you are so good at that."

"Not God, baby, just me. Tell me what it feels like." His mouth returned to her core.

"I...I can't talk." She struggled to form those three simple words. Her mind couldn't think beyond feeling the pleasure he gave her.

"Yes you can, Tabby."

"I feel the heat of your breath, the moisture of your tongue."

"What else?" Each time he spoke, he pulled away just far enough to speak then his mouth returned to her body, teasing her towards the climax building in her body.

"My whole body feels sensitive. I can feel myself climbing higher and higher, like I'm soaring toward a goal that is just out of reach." Tabby pried her hands from the blanket and grasped Nico's head. His hair felt silky as she thread it through her fingers, the strands slightly damp. That turned her on more. He was working hard to give her what she wanted.

"Are you ready to reach your goal, Tabby? Do you want to finish?"

"Yes, Nico." She couldn't stop herself from moving her hips to the rhythm he set with his tongue. She felt him flick her clitoris, once, twice, three times before her body exploded into tiny pieces. "Wow." She lay there panting, not caring how she looked, her body spent but still ready for more.

Nico eased up to look her in the face, his cocky grin in place. "See what you've been missing this whole time?" he said with a wink.

"Yes. I'd like to see more." Tabby started to pull his shirt up, her skin rubbing his warm, taunt back as she went. Her brazen response made her smile. She loved the playful side that Nico brought out in her.

"Now you're talking. Damn I love being undressed by a woman." Nico rolled off her onto his back. He looked so sexy laying there waiting for her. His messy hair, seductive eyes with those long, dark eyelashes. The tingle in her body started to grow again.

She lifted his shirt higher. His six-pack abs peeked out at her. Lowering her head she placed kisses across his stomach. Nico took over for a minute lifting just enough to pull the shirt up and over his head. A light dusting of black hair graced his impressive chest muscles. His tight skin a golden brown that spoke of his Italian heritage.

She kissed him again going higher and higher. He tasted of warm, passionate man. "Pants, baby. Get the pants." His strong hands caressed her back tickling her skin.

"You in a hurry?" she asked in a mischievous tone. Really she was too but she couldn't pass on the chance to give him a hard time.

"I'm so hard right now these pants are killing me. I need to feel you, skin to skin, your hot hungry body on top of mine. Your eyes on me, your hands, your tight body wrapped around me."

Damn how did he do that? He brought her to the brink with just a few words. She'd never known this kind of passion, this kind of sexual relationship and freedom that she was starting to feel with Nico. It wasn't about love; it was about enjoying each other and to her surprise that turned her on.

She reached for the button on his pants. After two shaky tries she pulled the button from the hole before tackling the zipper. The bulge in his pants was huge. She couldn't wait to see what waited for her when she finished undressing him. Tabby pulled his pants down his legs. When she reached his feet he kicked out of them. "Come on, baby. One more layer to go."

His voice sounded so raw, seductive. He didn't need to flirt, didn't need lines and jokes right now. His desire was obvious. It wasn't a game right now, just two people who needed to lose themselves in pleasure. Tabby couldn't pull her eyes away from the spot his thick erection bulged beneath his dark blue, snug-fitting boxer-briefs. His body jutted forward lifting his underwear up then back down again.

"Come on, Tabby. You keep looking at me like that and I'm going to lose control and embarrass myself."

She licked her lips anxious to finally get Nico undressed. Her hands followed the same trail, pulling his boxer-briefs down his legs, his impressive erection springing free. He kicked himself free while she stared. Her eyes couldn't part from the large shaft that rest against his belly.

"Like what you see, Tabby?" He tweaked her nipple. "I sure as hell do. You're so sexy, so alluring. I can't wait to be buried to the hilt inside your body. Come up here."

Tabby could do nothing but obey. Her legs straddled his body, her crotch resting against his as she lowered her head and kissed his lips. Nico took over immediately, running the show, setting the tempo with his mouth. His hand grabbed the back of her head, deepening the kiss. Their bodies were moist with sweat, her heart drumming loudly against her chest. As if on auto pilot her body began to rock against his.

"Hold up," he somehow reached his pants to pull a condom from his wallet. "I'm too primed for you, baby. I can feel your wetness. It makes me want to come right now." He ripped open the foil packet before reaching between their bodies to sheath himself. When he was covered he inserted one finger, then another inside her. A soft moan escaped her lips at the immediate pleasure. "So tight, so wet, so ready," he whispered before withdrawing his fingers and plunging inside her in one swift movement.

"Fuck." He'd never felt as good as he did buried in Tabby's wet heat. Her body held his cock tightly, like a glove. Perfect fucking fit. Better than he imagined. So good he almost couldn't move. Almost. Grabbing her silky smooth arms he pulled her down towards him so that her firm, brown breasts dangled in his face. He flexed, tenderly kissed each nipple then flipped her so that she lay under him.

He started to thrust deep inside her. A surprised, "Oh" rush from her lips as if the pleasure shocked her body. Then she caught his rhythm and moved with him. Damn she felt good. His body burned with intensity as he thrust in and out of her silky heat like this was the last time he was ever going to get laid in his life. "You feel un-fucking-believable, Tabby."

Looking down he saw her smile a shy smile while he continued moving, her breasts bouncing as he rode her. He almost came, right then and there. Struggling, Nico held himself back. He needed to make sure Tabby received the pleasure she deserved before he took his own. He was a man on a mission. A man who wanted to prove that they were good together in bed. He didn't want this to be a onetime shot. Knowing Tabby, it would be. He wasn't what she looked for

Unexpected Mr. Right   **99**

and for the first time in his life that thought made him a little bit sad.

Not right now though. He'd think about that later. Now he wanted to enjoy this. Enjoy her. "You're so tight, Baby," he thrust inside her feeling her body begin to clamp around him. She was so close. He leaned down close to her ear. "You're skin is so silky, your body so delicious. I'm going to devour you over and over before this night is done. Does that sound good to you?"

"Yes," her voice came out a hushed whisper. He could hardly make her words out. Hell yeah. He loved knowing he gave her such pleasure.

"Come for me, baby." His lips went for hers. The second he touched her she went over the edge, screaming his name against his mouth. He couldn't hold back any longer. He surged inside her once more, his body exploding with the ferocity of a bomb.

He collapsed on top of her, their heavy breathing mixing together, her heart pounding so strongly he felt it against his chest. She'd been everything he imagined, fire, passion, skill, everything. When he turned and rolled off her his body felt the loss immediately. He loved having a warm, spent woman under him. *This warm, spent woman is more like it.*

She turned her head to look at him. Her eyes looked heavy, like she would pass out at any second when she said, "Now I see what all the fuss is about, Nico. I never realized a one night stand could feel so exhilarating." Then she closed her eyes and drifted to sleep.

Did he just hear her right? Nico lay there, sleep eluding him. Her last words to him played over and over in his head. It pissed him off that she automatically assumed that's what tonight was about. But why should she think any different? That's what Nico did, have flings and one night stands. He never hid the fact; he'd propositioned her with them many times in the past.

A one night stand never felt like what they'd just shared. This was different, deeper, more intense. God, he'd wanted her for so long and now that he had her he wasn't satisfied. He wanted more, crazy as it sounded. Something about her clicked with him, she felt right, like they should be sharing a lot more than just one, two, or even three nights together.

For the first time he wanted more. He probably always had with her but just didn't know it. Now he did. The thought should scare the crap out of him but it didn't. He wasn't ready to swear his undying love but he did want to call her his. To be able to tell guys like Lance to fuck off and stay the hell away from her. He wanted the right to kiss her, touch her, and make love to her anytime he felt like it. Hell he wanted to date her, bring her to movies, picnics the whole nine yards.

For the first time in his life Nico wanted to have an actual relationship with a woman. How that happened he didn't know. Now he had to find a way to convince Tabby, who thought he was a one night stand kind of man, that he wanted more. He'd have to convince a woman who longed to have a relationship, just not with a guy like him, that he was the man she should have one with.

He'd have to take it slow, that he knew. Tabby made sure to be cautious. She'd never believe him unless he worked her into the idea, spent more time with her.

Holy shit. How did he get himself into this mess?

Tabby's tired eyes struggled, flittering back and forth between open and closed. A heavy ache throbbed between her legs; her body lay limp out of shear exhaustion. A warm, male body nestled behind her back. Nico. He'd been amazing last night. So different from any of the men she'd been with before. He engaged all her senses. Pleasured every inch of her body. Showed her that all the practice he engaged in really paid off.

And she just added her name to his list. A wave of nausea formed in her stomach as her heart accelerated in excitement. She didn't know what emotion was the strongest. Last night she did something she never wanted to do. Have a one night

Unexpected Mr. Right   **101**

stand. And the sad part is, she didn't think she regretted it.

When Nico moved behind her, burying his face in her neck, her body thrummed to life. Apparently the escapade was something her body wanted to do again. But then, that wouldn't be a one night stand would it? Maybe a two night stand? Ah, hell, what was she doing? She had no idea how to react to him when he woke up. She didn't know what to do.

What she did know is she wanted him again. She enjoyed herself, she enjoyed Nico last night. Like everything he did, he made love with passion, with a fiery excitement he had inside him like no one she'd ever known. Her body wanted him, her head told her it was a mistake. This wasn't her. This wasn't what she wanted.

"Stop thinking so much." His voice was low, gravely. He sounded as tired as she felt.

"How did you know?"

"You're stiff as a board. Loosen up and stop over-thinking last night."

"That's easy for you to say," she rolled quickly to face him. Her lips stopped inches from his mouth. He leaned in. Her heart lurched as if trying to escape her chest. He moved in closer. Oh God, he was going to kiss her and she would let him.

"Don't worry," he said a breath away from her. "I'm not going to kiss you. Not until we talk."

Well damn.

"Now tell me why you're so stressed out. Otherwise, I might have to kiss you again. And I won't stop there, Tabby. Maybe you need another round to loosen you up again. What do you think?" His voice was now smooth as honey. Amazing how he could turn on the charm like that. And it worked. Wetness began form at the junction of her thighs.

Temptation almost pushed the word yes from her mouth. It bubbled in her throat but she held herself in check. "I've never done this before, Nico. While it was fun, exciting and the best sex I've ever had, it's going to take me a while to get used to. I have no idea how to act. Usually when I'm in bed with a man we have a relationship, the possibility of falling in love and settling down together. All the things you're completely against."

"The best sex you've ever had, huh?" He put his arm around her, his fingers tickling her back.

"Nico."

"I'm kidding. Trying to lighten the mood a little bit. You're too depressed for someone who had 'the best sex she's ever had'."

She shot him a warning look. Her eyes narrowed telling him now wasn't the time. She wanted him to take this serious. For her it was very serious.

"We have a relationship, Slugger, just not the kind you're used to. Last I checked we're friends, right?"

"Yeah."

"Okay then. That solves that issue. Second, I'm not against people falling in love and settling down, I'm just not sure it's for me. There's nothing wrong with that."

"But that's what I want, Nico. I'm not saying I'm in love with you or I want us to settle down together but no matter how good this felt, my ultimate goal is forever, not just a night or two. You want to steer clear of that. The two just don't mix." She hated saying this. Her body wanted nothing more than to engage in a fling with Nico.

Nico pulled away from her and sat up. His hand immediately ruffling his already mussed hair. A deep breath escaped his body. "That's not what you're looking for right now. You said so yourself. Right now you want to have fun, to prove to yourself you can spend time with a guy, who would be me and me alone," he said sounding a bit territorial.

"Without ending up with a broken heart. Since I'm obviously completely wrong for you as you've told me time and time again, you know you have no risk losing your heart. Then we both win, baby. We're great together. Why deny ourselves that pleasure? Who knows where it will lead us?"

She noticed he called her Slugger when they played around, when they were sexual, she turned into Baby.

He leaned down toward her on the bed. Oh yeah, they were

Unexpected Mr. Right   **103**

good together. Her nipples perked to attention under his intense stare. "I have to tell you, I'm not done with you yet. You said you want some kind of relationship? We can have that. We're friends, good friends what happen to enjoy each other in bed. I'm not ready to give you up yet." He kissed her, the touch of his lips soft.

"We can do everything together normal people in a relationship do. Hell, we already are. Give us a chance, Tabby. Give me a chance. I'm really not as bad as you seem to think I am."

She pulled away, guilt assaulting her. "I know I've given you a hard time in the past but it was just because I'm attracted to you and I didn't want to admit it. I know you're not a bad guy. We just want different things."

"I think we want the same things. We both want each other. I know I'm not the right guy for you forever, but I'm right for now. We have too much fun together for it to be any other way."

He was right. She wanted him. She didn't want to give this up yet and why should she? They were both adults. Both friends who she thought could still be friends once they ended whatever it was they were doing. He could go back to his life and she'd go back to hers. Right now, they could pretend they both wanted the same thing. "Can we really do this? The whole friends with benefits thing?"

He buried his face in her neck, kissing the tender spot behind her ear. "It's more than that, Baby. It's a relationship, just not the conventional kind. I'm not a conventional kind of guy."

Didn't she know it? Arching her head back to give him better access, she wrapped her arms around him, pulling him down on her. Without direction from her, her body started to move against his. "Yes, Nico. I want this."

"There's only one problem."

Tabby stopped moving. She somehow gotten used to the idea of their "relationship" fast. Fear tickled her spine wondering what he had to say. "What?" a nervous quiver shook her voice.

Nico looked at her, winked, and said, "I don't have another condom."

Chapter Eight

That hadn't gone quite as planned. Nico plopped onto his living room couch, his hands ruffled his hair before he again rose and started to pace the room. She had him off balance, like he teetered on the edge of a cliff, or at a crossroads to something major he just didn't know what it was. And that confused the shit out of him. Women never confused him. He prided himself on knowing just what women wanted. Until Tabby.

The woman had fire burning in her veins, if she'd just acknowledge it. She was passionate, funny and fine as hell. Too bad she seemed to think he was such a womanizing asshole. How he'd gotten that rep, he didn't know. It pissed him off that the people around him labeled him that. He never played games, he enjoyed his bachelorhood but always on the up and up with whomever he was with at the time.

Obviously he gave everyone the wrong idea about himself. Just because he never chose to have a relationship in the past didn't mean he wasn't able. It meant he hadn't found a woman who made him burn, made him ache, in ways beyond the little Nic in his pants. Now that he found that woman his past kept her at bay. Made the man who wanted to give a relationship a try for the first time settle for the lame story of friends with benefits he laid out for her.

She'd need proof he could be the man she wanted. Hell, he

wasn't saying forever, but they both deserved to give this a try. He'd show her Mr. Wrong could be Mr. Right. That she'd looked for the wrong kind of man in the past. Whether she wanted to admit it or not, she liked his flirtatious, fun-loving ways. She didn't want the stiffs she thought she did. Oh, yeah, he'd show her what she really wanted. And if he lost his heart in the process, well, that wasn't as scary as he thought it would be.

Tabby, Kaylee and Bri walked through the florist shop, the scents of the different flowers wafting over them. Kaylee needed to finalize her arrangements for the wedding. It should have been done weeks ago, since the wedding date would be upon them in a short couple weeks, but since Kaylee didn't want big arrangements it wouldn't be a big deal. She'd always loved flowers. In high school she helped her neighbor, who was a florist, in her shop on the weekends. Kaylee asked her if she'd make the arrangements and she'd been happy to say yes.

"What about these?" Bri asked pointing to a loud purple flower that she'd never even seen before. It was unique, that's for sure but not for a wedding.

"They have to be yellow, dork," Tabby teased. "Remember when she chose yellow for her color?"

"You know me, I like to throw a little pizzazz into things. It's not my fault the two of you are boring," she said with a smile. The three girls laughed. They loved giving each other a hard time out of fun. They all loved and respected one another too much to take offense.

"No purple pizzazz in my wedding, girl. I want something simple. I'm thinking about a small arrangement of daisies."

"I like it. I think that fits you, Kaylee. We can get fresh daisy's, tie simple yellow ribbon around them, you know something like that, delicate, simple, but pretty." The wheels turned in Tabby's head. This would be fun. She couldn't wait. "I'll have to make yours a little bigger. We'll want your arrangement to stand out next to me and the purple pizzazz over there."

"Hey," Bri swatted her. "Don't knock my flowers."

Kaylee laughed. "We're not knocking them but you aren't carrying those things in my wedding either."

"You guys are no fun." Then changing the subject, Bri said, "So are we done here? Do you have enough to work some magic, Tab? I'm starved. We should grab something to eat."

"Pizza sounds good," Kaylee added.

Tabby groaned. "You guys would have been so proud of me. I made the best pizza with Nico the other night." Her heart dropped. The second the words fell from her mouth she realized she made a mistake. Bri and Kaylee both stopped walking and stared at her. Kaylee's eyes were huge in surprise, Bri smirked a knowing smile. *Shit*. Looks like Lucy had some splanin' to do.

"Screw the food," Bri said. "We're going to your place. I need details."

It amazed her they waited until they got to her house before they asked any questions. First she thought she'd use the time to think of an excuse but she didn't. She wasn't doing anything wrong so why hide it? Kaylee and Brianna would do the same thing, hell they had done the same thing so why should she hide in the corner? For the first time she threw caution to the wind and followed her hormones rather than her heart. It felt damn good.

Not only that but she missed talking to her girls. Holding this in hadn't been easy, especially now that they'd slept together. Sex just wasn't the same without girl talk. She wouldn't give them the step by step, but she had to share something. She almost burst at the seams holding it in.

"Talk," Bri ordered when they walked inside and all took seats in her living room.

"Usually I'd tell Bri to have a little patience but I'm with her on this one, Tab. Time to spill," Kaylee gave a look that said if she tried to avoid the questions they'd use force if necessary. She didn't doubt the gleam in her best friend's eyes.

"I love being the one with a secret," Tabby teased. "Usually I want information on your private lives. Mine isn't usually the exciting one."

"Well now it is so get to talkin'," Bri told her.

For the first time in her life, Tabby felt like a bad girl. Like she was about to share some forbidden, naughty secret. She'd done something just for herself, had something just for herself. An illicit affair that had nothing to do with promises of forever. Sure, she still wanted forever but that isn't what this was about. This was about a friend who she felt comfortable enough with to explore the sexual being inside her that had never burned as brightly as it did when Nico touched her.

"I'm talking. Chill out." Tabby filled her lungs with air before exhaling deeply. "A couple weeks ago Nico showed up at my house after dinner on Friday. He made me realize what a bitch I'd been to him lately."

"Thank God for that. You really did give Super Chef a hard time, girl," Bri stated honestly coating her words.

"I know. Don't make me feel any worse. Anyway, he brought up spending time together, getting to know each other more but just as friends, ya know? At first I was leery, I thought it was just a ploy to get into my pants but he seemed sincere and I realized it was something I had to do.

"Any man I've ever been close with I had a romantic relationship with, I pursued the relationship hoping, thinking that he may be the one. Honestly, I felt a little pathetic. I'd never had a close male friend before. I needed to prove to myself that I could have one and that I could get close to a guy without falling in love and getting my heart broken."

Tabby stretched and wondered how much she should tell them. She felt bad not talking with Nico first. They'd promised to keep their "friendship" on the down low. Once Bri and Kaylee knew, it would no longer be the secret they'd agreed to. "So, we've been hanging out ever since. He's teaching me to cook, too," she said with a smile.

"Did you get laid?" Bri's eyes held hers not letting her escape the question.

Well, that settled the how much to tell them problem. She couldn't lie, they'd see right through her. Plus, she kind of wanted to tell them, Nico was too good not to share. Not figuratively speaking. "Yes," she said her eyes glancing down.

Charming jumped on Kaylee's lap and she started to pet him. "Don't start getting sheepish on us now. How'd it go from friends to sex? Are you guys seeing each other? Are you sure you're not going to get hurt?" Kaylee fired questions at her one after another.

"Give her a chance to reply, Kay. Tabby's finally grown some balls and I want to hear about it."

"Hey. I've always had balls!" As soon as the words left her mouth she realized how foolish they sounded.

Bri looked at her, smiled and said, "I bet Nico was pretty damn surprised when he discovered that."

Laughter erupted from all three women. Deep, belly laughs that you could only get from spending time with your girls. Well, and Nico. He made her laugh like no one could. He did a lot of things like no one could. Once her laughter calmed enough to speak, Tabby said, "You know what I mean. You better stop giving me a hard time if you want to hear the rest of this story."

They both quieted enough that the only sound in the room came from Charming. He purred in pleasure as Kaylee stroked his head. "Friday night he woke me up pounding on my door like the damn world was coming to an end. The second I opened it he pounced, kissing me, touching me. It almost like he *couldn't* keep his hands off me even if he wanted to. Like he had to have me. I don't know what came over him but it felt too good to deny."

"Jealous," Bri and Kaylee said at the same time.

Tabby shook her head at the crazy suggestion. "What is there to be jealous about? It's not like I have a man, or even a prospect for goodness sakes. Plus, jealousy means feeling more than just sexual attraction. Besides friendship, there is nothing between us beyond overpowering sexual attraction."

"Hello? Lance? He totally wanted you and Nico knew it. He's staking his claim." Bri looked proud of herself when she spoke.

"Don't be ridiculous." That didn't make any sense whatsoever.

"I love you, Tab, but for a chick who wants a man so bad, you really don't know jack about them." Her eyes were teasing, a smirk tilted her lips.

If she didn't love her friend so much and know her words came from the heart, she just might have given them a whole new reason to call her slugger.

A couple hours later, Tabby sat curled up on her couch tossing buttery popcorn into her mouth, an old romance movie on TV. She wasn't paying attention to the movie, instead she nuzzled deeper into the soft fabric of her couch and let out a sigh. Though Bri seemed happy about her little tryst with Nico, Kaylee hadn't been so optimistic. She worried about her heart getting involved. She worried about her getting hurt.

Not that she could blame her friend for her fear. Tabby's track record proved her most likely to be right but this felt different. Nico felt different. She put up a mental roadblock to that kind of thinking. Nico wasn't different, she was. This whole relationship wasn't about 'the dream'. She put that on hold for the first time in her life and decided to focus on herself, on her friends, and on enjoying her very new friendship with Nico.

Pride filled her. For the first time in a long while she felt proud of the path her life took. Why shouldn't she enjoy her sexuality? Men did it all the time. They were being safe and they both knew the score so no one would get hurt. Nico tried to tell her that so many times in the past. Why hadn't she listened sooner? A whole lot of hassle and misunderstanding

Unexpected Mr. Right 111

would have been prevented if she had.

Not much she could do about it now. Inhaling a deep breath, Tabby sucked in the delicious smell of the popcorn before placing the bowl on her table. She had enough for one night. The buttery taste wasn't what she really wanted. She really hungered for Nico. Again. On Saturday morning, after he broke the news that he didn't have any more condoms, they'd talked a few minutes more before she remembered a meeting and had to shoo him out the door.

The toe-curling kiss goodbye he laid on her at the door held her over for a little while. Now she wanted him again. Tabby giggled to herself at the irony. The man tried and tried to get her in the sack for months and she did nothing but deny him. Now, she lay on her couch, sensitive, for the one thing he'd tried for so long to give her. Thank God she finally listened.

The shrill ring of her phone jarred her from her musings. Tabby picked up the phone from the table by her couch, clicked the talk button and said, "Hello".

"Hey, Slugger." Nico's lazy drawl echoed through the phone. Her nipples puckered at the sound of his voice.

"Hey. You must be psychic. I was just thinking about you." She wouldn't tell him exactly what she thought. Proving him right wasn't on her list of things to do for the day. The less he knew about her still burning desire for him the better.

"Thinking about what I can do to you? What I'm going to do to you again? I haven't thought of another damn thing since I left you, Baby. I burned my damn lunch today. That's never happened before."

The thought tickled her from the tips of her toes to the top of her head. She liked knowing how much she affected him. Liked knowing this uncontrollable attraction wasn't one sided. "Hm, if you're burning food, I might have to look elsewhere for a new cooking teacher. I want to learn from the best, you know?"

"I am the best. You won't find anyone who can show you all I have planned in store for you, *Tesoro*. You can bank on that."

The seductive edge in his voice made her squirm. Right into

the couch wishing him there to show her exactly what he spoke about.

"Why do I have the feeling we aren't talking about cooking anymore?" she asked.

"Because I'm not."

Oh boy. Better not start something they couldn't finish. Not unless he could come over at least. She wanted to ask him but she didn't want to sound needy but quickly changed her mind. He knew her well enough to know she wasn't dependent upon him. They'd spent time together for a few weeks and she wouldn't have hesitated to ask him over before so she should now. "Are you coming over?"

A groan erupted through the phone. She could sense his desire strumming through the deep sound. "I wish I could. I'd like nothing more than to come over and continue where we left off but I have do my final fitting for the wedding and then we're going to Luciano's. He wants to go over some restaurant stuff with me since he'll be on his honeymoon in a few weeks."

Each nerve ending in her eager body deflated.

"I can cancel on the beer," he told her. "Spending the night with you sounds a lot more fun."

"No, no, don't do that. We aren't in a relationship; you don't have to bail on your cousin to make time for me. I'm sure you have important wedding business to take care of."

He exhaled what sounded like a frustrated breath. "If I had plans with anyone other than Luciano, if it wasn't so important, I'd be there in a heartbeat, Tabby. Nothing could keep me away."

She smiled. Her body warmed even though she knew it shouldn't. Everything about him made her feel good about herself. "We'll do it another time." He laughed and she didn't have to ask to know why he snickered.

"Yes, we will do it again. I'm ready to bust at the seams to have you again. Do you have plans for tomorrow?"

"Tomorrow's crazy for me. I'm not sure I'll be able to break away from work until late." They went back and forth until they realized both were booked solid until their usual Friday at

Luciano's get together. They hadn't been spending so much time together for very long but she realized at that moment that she'd quickly become used to their friendship and the fun they had together. She'd miss spending time with him, miss the playful banter that they shared.

The importance of his friendship struck her like a jolt of electricity. She didn't want to do anything to sacrifice their friendship and from what she'd seen in the past the whole friends with benefits thing rarely worked in the end. He assured her they'd be fine the other day but she needed another confirmation. "Are you sure we're doing the right thing here, Nico? Will we still be able to be friends after this is done?"

He didn't hesitate with his reply. "What we're doing couldn't be more right, *Tesoro*. We're taking our friendship to new heights and nothing will change that. You're stuck with me." He added the last part with the unique playful dance to his tone that he alone possessed.

"Not stuck. We're buddies, Nico. Your friendship means a lot to me." More than she thought it would. When it came to Nico she was quickly realizing he had more qualities than met the eye.

He sat quiet a minute then said, "I have to go, Slugger. Talk to you soon."

"Wait," she called into the phone. "What does *Tesoro* mean?" she almost forgot to ask.

"Treasure," he said simply before she heard a click and the line go dead. Pulling the phone away from her ear, Tabby looked at it like she could see Nico through the receiver. *Weird.* He never hung up that abruptly. The edge she'd heard in his voice made her wonder if everything was okay. Dismissing the thought from her head, Tabby stood up and put in an exercise video. She needed to keep herself busy somehow.

Buddies? What the hell? Nico never experienced a woman he'd slept with calling him her buddy. He didn't like it, especially coming from Tabby. She had somehow woven her way into his life to become an integral part of his world and not as a damn buddy. More like a puzzle piece that fit together to make a whole picture. He shook his head. Now she had him sounding like a goddamn woman comparing puzzle pieces to their lives.

Get it together Valenti.

"What's your problem?" Luciano asked as they sat in his office a little while later. They were supposed to be going over the work Luciano would need him to do while he took his honeymoon yet Nico hadn't heard a word he said. If he even said anything yet.

"How do you know something's wrong?"

"You haven't responded to a thing I've said. You're grunting and groaning over there like you have a severe case of indigestion. However, I think yours goes by a different name. Something a little more feminine perhaps."

The gleam in Luciano's eye told him his cousin enjoyed this way too much. Not that he could blame him. He'd given Luciano shit when he started falling in love with Kaylee. *Wow. Where the hell did that come from?* He wasn't falling in love with Tabby. He liked her, he wanted her but that's about all. "Ah shit, Lu," Nico ran a hand through his hair. "I don't know what the hell is wrong with me."

"Well I know you slept with her. Did you feel a little more than you thought you would?"

Nico looked at him wide-eyed. "How do you know about that?"

Luciano laughed. "You know how women are. Tabby told Kaylee. She couldn't hold it in so she told me. She's worried about her. I told her she didn't need to be. Am I right?"

Hell, maybe he should just tell Luciano what was going on. Well, if he knew what was going on it would be a lot easier. He didn't understand where all the crazy thoughts in his head came from or what they meant. Luciano might be able to help him make some sense out of his sudden desire to have a relationship. But then he'd see the same smug grin he'd dished

Unexpected Mr. Right   115

out to his cousin about Kaylee returned to him. He didn't want that. No reason he couldn't make sense of this himself.

If it were love, he'd know it. Wouldn't he? He saw it everyday when he looked at his parents, his sisters, his family. Tabby meant a lot to him, the woman was fine as hell and had a great personality to boot, but he wasn't in love with her. He also wasn't ready to end whatever it was they were doing. "Naw, I'm not going to hurt her. I may not know what the hell I'm doing, but can tell you I'd never hurt, Tab."

Luciano gave Nico a wicked grin that told him his cousin thought he knew more than he did. "Don't go looking at me like that. It's not what you think. The woman has me tied in knots. For the first time in my life I'm flustered by the opposite sex but it isn't what you're thinking." Is it?

"How the tables have turned, Nic. I thought you were supposed to be all knowing when it came to women."

Luciano enjoyed this way too much. Not that he faulted him. He'd be doing the same thing if the situation were reversed. "I know all the ways to pleasure a woman, I can tell you that," he said with a smile. "It's the other shit that's getting to me."

Luciano turned serious. "Like what? She's just another woman, right? Nothing special."

Nico didn't have to think before answering the question. He fought the rise in the heat of his blood by Luciano thinking such a thing. He felt primal like he had to protect her. "What the hell do you mean by that? Tabby is far from average. She means more to me than any other woman I've ever know. Hell, she's the first woman I've ever wanted to have an actual relationship with. And the kicker is, I'm tricking her into it. Tabby, the woman who has wanted to settle down her whole life and I have to trick her into a damn relationship. She's got it in her head that I'm this heartbreaker that leaves a trail of women in my wake."

The smile stretching across Luciano's face told Nico he just fell into a trap set by his know-it-all cousin. He spilled his guts when he hadn't planned on it. "Fuck." Nico stood and paced the office. "I want her, Lu. I really do. I'm not ready for the whole, 'do you take this woman to be your lawfully wedded wife' bit but she's different. I don't want to let her go right now and I don't know if I ever will. How the hell did I get myself into this mess?"

Luciano stood up, pat him on the back and said, "We need to get ourselves a drink, Cousin. Then I can explain a few things to you."

Damn, for the first time in his life Nico had to get woman advice. Might as well take him out and shoot him now. He lost his touch.

Chapter Nine

The week stretched on, one busy day after another for Tabby. Work picked up, the wedding date inched closer and closer. One thing piled on top of another until Friday finally came. Bone tired exhaustion gripped Tabby's limbs but she needed her night out. Needed to see her friends, have a drink, and let her hair down. And she wanted to see Nico. He'd been in the back of her mind trying to push through until finally she gave in and thought about nothing but him all week long.

She needed a good laugh, a good time and Nico gave that to her like no one else in her life. That knowledge should put her on edge but right now it didn't. Right now she just wanted to bask in this new found freedom she'd given herself. Freedom that he'd given her. Surprisingly, the decision to halt her search for Mr. Right released a weight on her chest that she hadn't known resided there.

Walking into the dimly lit atmosphere of Luciano's Tabby felt at home. This place had somehow grown to mean so much to her. Like a second home, a place she and her girls could come to have a good time and be around their new found friends. For Kaylee, the place she met the man of her dreams. Still, even though she enjoyed what she had right now, Tabby still looked forward to that day herself. She wondered where she would find him. Where their story would take place.

"Hey Slugger," Nico rounded the corner and walked up to

her. He didn't wear his chef whites like he usually did on Friday nights. He looked sexy as sin in a pair of blue jeans, black t-shirt, and his tousled hair. For the first time since she met him, his face wasn't cleanly shaven, he had a dark, five o'clock shadow dusting his jaw line.

Damn. This man oozed sexiness in a way that should be illegal. He made her want to do all sorts of forbidden things to him. With him. "Hey there. What's up? Why aren't you dressed for work?" They walked together towards their table. His arm brushed against hers making it damn near impossible not jump him right there. His heat scorched her arm, shooting flames of desire throughout her body.

"I got my shift covered. I was thinking, since we've both had such a crazy week and haven't been able to get together we should take advantage when we can." He stopped then lowered his mouth to her ear. "We have time to make up for. I plan to ravage you, Tabby." He pulled away and winked, "in a friendly way of course."

She wanted to come right there. Right in the middle of Luciano's and who cared who watched her. "Friends with benefits." Her body suddenly drained of her tiredness. Excitement coursed through her muscles that minutes ago ached with wariness. Soon she'd be able to cash in the benefit she'd been thinking about all week.

He leaned toward her and she thought he was going to kiss her when he said, "Bri, Kaylee and Luciano can't take their eyes off us," he nodded toward the table. "We better join them before they get too many wild ideas in their heads."

She had enough of those in her own mind for all of them.

"So what's up with you two?" Brianna asked halfway through dinner. "I know you're getting it on but are we going to be planning another wedding in the future? You Valenti men seem to have a thing for us sistas."

Tabby felt the choke come on as she spit her drink out.

Damn, Brianna pushed her into having a Kaylee moment. Before she got together with Luciano she couldn't be in his presence without dropping, spilling or spitting something. "Brianna! I can't believe you just said that. Nothing is going on between Nico and I."

"Now that's not true, Slugger. Something is definitely going on between us."

"Nothing serious."

"Say's who?" Nico smiled at her.

Tabby couldn't be more surprised by his words. "Says us."

"Says you."

Words escaped her. What did he mean? Knowing Nico, he was having fun trying to give Bri a show since she called them out so bluntly. But still, he looked so serious she couldn't be sure.

"I think I'd have to agree with Nico on this one," Luciano added. "You two look like a couple to me." He nodded toward her. Tabby looked behind her to see Nico's arm around her on the back of the chair.

"Am I on candid camera or something?" This so didn't make sense. Nico talked like he wanted more than just their friends with benefits arrangement. Luciano acted like he knew something she didn't and Bri, well, she was being herself but not the rest of them.

"No you're not on candid camera but I do think you're in denial." Brianna took a sip of her drink. "Pretty soon I'm going to be the only single person at this table."

Tabby pushed the key in her lock with a nervous hand. Why her nerves decided to kick in tonight she hadn't a clue. But they did. As she opened the door to her apartment she couldn't help but think about what they'd talked about at dinner tonight. What Luciano said. What Nico said. She couldn't make sense of it. No matter how many times she tried to remind herself they were just friends, friends who happened to sleep together, but friends all the same, the shoe just didn't fit. Tonight felt different.

The reason why escaped her. She knew where they stood, knew they wanted different things in life but for the first time she found herself wishing they could meet in the middle somewhere. She blocked that thought from her conscience. She wasn't there yet, but she had a feeling Nico could be a man she'd fall in love with. Real love, not the wishful façade she felt in the past.

"I'm exhausted." Tabby put her purse on the table. "I had such a long week."

"Yeah, me too, Slugger."

After stepping into her kitchen, Tabby opened the fridge and pulled out a bottle of wine. "Do you want a glass?"

Nico shrugged. "Sounds good to me. While you get that I'm going to use your restroom real quick."

He left the room. Tabby opened the wine bottle and poured the wine into their glasses. She needed to relax tonight but she also wanted Nico. Her body pulsed at the thought of having him again. To her surprise she heard the water start in her bathroom. Seconds later Nico stepped into the kitchen a mischievous smile on his gorgeous face.

"You have a Jacuzzi tub."

Oh boy. "I know."

"That's the perfect way for us to start our night, Slugger. Grab the bottle and I'll get the wine glasses."

Her shakiness returned but whether it originated because of fear or excitement she couldn't tell. Both emotions bubbled in her body like a pot with water boiling over the edges. She felt that same amount of heat as well. Tabby carried the bottle of wine and followed Nico into her bathroom. Her oversized, Jacuzzi tub sat half filled, her candles were lit, the lights off making the room dim and sensual.

Nico set the glasses on the thick edge of the tub before turning off the water. He twisted around to face her. "This will be even better than our night on the phone, *Tesoro*." He took the bottle from her hand and placed it next to the wine glasses.

Unexpected Mr. Right

"My hands will really be on you, touching you, rubbing you." His words made her tingle like his hands were already doing what she knew would come shortly. He reached out to her and started to unbutton her blouse. She shivered in anticipation.

Nico lowered the blouse off her shoulders and let it drop to the floor. She stood in front of him in her white lace bra and skirt. Leaning toward her he kissed the crease between her neck and shoulder. Tabby took a deep breath and inhaled his musky, masculine scent. Nico kissed his way down her neck, he stopped to lick the swell of her breasts. A moan ripped from the back of her throat.

Then he nipped at her breast through the lace of her bra while his hands worked at the latch in the back. "I like lace almost as much as I like silk but this has to go." With a flick her bra unlatched, Nico quickly discarded it on the floor with her shirt.

"You're amazing, Tabby. Do you know that?"

She felt the warmth of his mouth around her nipple. An aching need pounded inside every inch of her. She didn't answer. Nico switched breasts, this time his skillful, wet tongue flicked her peak, he rolled her other nipple between two fingers of one hand when she felt his other hand try and ease down the zipper on her skirt.

"I want you naked but I want to touch you at the same time. I can't keep my hands off your sexy body." He was a talker and it turned her on even more. She'd never been with someone who talked as much as Nico did during foreplay or sex. His voice so filled with lust, with urgency built the pleasure in her body to new heights. Both his hands moved to her back, skimming up and down her bare skin tickling her and fueling the pulsing throb between her legs.

"That was a hint, Tabby." His breath heated her breast, his hands still rubbed her back, her side, her shoulders. "Take off your skirt." His words were an order but one she didn't mind to obey. She felt the lick of his tongue at her nipple before he sucked it deeply into his mouth. The pleasure zooming through her whole body almost made her forget his command to take off her skirt. But she didn't. She wanted to get naked so he could touch her everywhere.

Tabby unzipped the side zipper on her skirt and it shimmied down her legs to join her other clothes on the linoleum floor. Nico stopped his movements, backed away, his eyes never left hers and smiled.

He needed another set of hands, another set of eyes, so he could touch and take in every gorgeous part of Tabby's body. She stood in front of him, beautiful mocha skin contrasting the white of her lacey panties, her cropped hair sexily disheveled from his hands, her arms hanging to her side. He'd never seen a more beautiful sight in his life. He wanted to take her in every way imaginable. She had his insides in knots and not just from the lust that overwhelmed his aching body. Something about her reached him on a deeper level.

Nico eyed the dark thatch of curls he saw behind he sexy, barley there panties. Unable to use any finesse at this moment he ripped the panties down her legs. Tabby stepped out to accommodate him. He sucked in a deep breath. His dick throbbed with the passionate need only Tabby could give him.

She sucked her lower lip into her mouth and watched him. Nico fought himself not to take her mouth again, not to reach out and bury his fingers inside her. First he needed to release his body from the constricting clothes that suddenly felt five sizes too small. And he wanted her to do it. Wanted to see her long, sexy, fingers on his body, taking off his clothes.

As if she could read his mind Tabby stepped forward and pulled his shirt up and over his head. Damn he wanted her. Next she lowered herself to the floor, pulling his button from the hole and lowering his pants and boxer-briefs down his legs. He loved watching her undress him. Loved seeing the unbridled passion in her eyes when she looked at his naked body. Then she did something he hadn't expected but it felt so right all he could do was moan when she cupped him, stroked

Unexpected Mr. Right

the length of him.

"Jesus, Tabby. Even your hands turn me inside out."

"You make me feel so incredibly sexy. When I'm with you I feel like a wanton woman who can tame even the most untamable man. No one has ever turned me on like you do, Nico."

Whatever grew between them was more than just turning each other on. He'd been turned on in the past. Nothing compared to what she did to him. He ached, burned, to possess her. She kissed the head of his cock and he almost died right there. He couldn't handle that. Not right now. He needed to touch her. "Not yet, baby. I'm dying to get my hands on you. To pleasure you." Pulling her to her feet, Nico kissed her. His tongue dove into her mouth telling her just how much he wanted her.

He stopped and stepped into the tub, bringing her with him. She sat between his legs, her back against his chest. Reminding himself that he wanted to make her feel good in every way he could, Nico started by rubbing her shoulders. She leaned against him, relaxed as he kneaded her muscles. Damn her silky soft skin felt right under his fingers. He could feel her melting under his touch, moans and sighs filled the air.

"You have magical hands, Nico."

He moved his magical hands to tease her breasts. A shocked gasp escaped her before she relaxed against him again. He cupped her mounds, rolled and pinched her nipples. "My hands where made to give you pleasure, baby. You're body made for me to touch." He was telling her what he wanted. Before this night ended he'd get Tabby to realize they should give this a shot. A real shot, not the friends with benefits crap she thought they had going right now. "I would do anything to make you happy, to make your body burst with satisfaction."

He lowered one hand beneath the water and cupped her between her legs. She opened them giving him better access. Without hesitation Nico plunged two fingers inside her. He pumped them in and out, her body matching his rhythm.

"Nico," she said breathlessly.

"Yes baby?" He kept his fingers going, his other hand still enjoying her breast.

"Oh my God you feel so good. I...I can hardly stand it."

"You can take whatever I give you, *Tesoro*. I love to feel your silky heat wrapped around my fingers, feel your body buck against mine. You're so hot, Tabby. So perfect. Don't doubt what you can handle."

She came apart in his arms, screaming his name, her body tightening around his fingers. His cock jutted against her backside with the sweet sound of her release. He almost came himself.

Her body sizzled. Intense fervor surged in her and now she lay against Nico's firm body, blissfully content. She felt his erection begin to move against her backside making her body purr to life. Despite the overpowering climax she just had she felt ready for another round. She wanted to feel him inside her again, filling her, stroking her to completion. He was an addictive pleasure that she couldn't deny herself. Not right now. "Take me to bed." Her voice came out a plea.

"I thought you'd never ask." Nico stood up lifting her in his strong arms in one fluid movement. On the way out he grabbed his pants and a towel from her rack. They never drank the wine, left the tub filled, and soaked her floor on their journey to her room but she didn't care. All that mattered right now was Nico and getting him inside her. Her body urgent for his touch.

"You have to stand up for a minute, baby." Nico set her on her feet before he quickly began to dry her. He didn't take his time, didn't touch her, she could see his enthusiasm in his movements, in his eyes. His laid back demeanor completely disappeared. Her body felt aware of his every movement. His quick brushes with the towel made her shiver in anticipation, when he dried himself she watched, waited until he would lay her down.

His olive skin was so was smooth yet masculine, his dark body hair added to his sexual allure. Veins showed in his hands, in his cock. Everything turned her on, she wanted to soak in the sight of him. Every part of him. He dropped the towel and grabbed condoms from his pants pocked throwing them on the bedside table. Nico sat on her bed and pulled her on top of him then leaned back, his head resting on the pillows.

"I want you to ride me, Tabby."

Her body shattered into a million different pieces at his request. Tabby leaned down and kissed him. Nico took over his tongue erotically intertwining with hers. Damn this man could kiss. She straddled him, her sex against his as his tongue dove in and out of her mouth. His hands roamed her body, caressing her into an extremely erotic state.

"Condom," he said against her mouth.

Tabby grabbed a condom package, ripped it open and then lowered it on his massively hard erection. He was so large, so long and thick. She sat up enough to get him into the right position before she lowered herself on him. He stretched her, filled her oh so right. Unable to hold back anymore Tabby started to move on top of him. Nico leaned up enough to suck one of her nipples into his mouth and she almost came right then and there.

"Hell, yeah, baby. You feel so good. I can't get enough of you."

She wanted to please him so she continued to rock on top of him. She stretched one arm out behind his head pushing him closer to her aching breasts. Nico moved with her, his tongue giving her just as much pleasure as his lower half. It was all too much, too consuming. Tabby felt herself shatter. Explosions ignited inside her as she called out his name. A couple strokes later she felt him join her in sexual bliss.

Tabby's limp body rolled over easily when Nico pulled her into his arms. She was spent. Her body damp with perspiration, her breaths coming out in shallow gasps. "I didn't think you'd be much of a cuddler."

He let out a small laugh. "I'm usually not. There's something different about you though. I want to feel every inch of your delectable body."

Now it was her turn to laugh. Oh she appreciated his efforts all right but there's no way he thought her any different than he did the other women he'd been with. What they had wasn't any different. *Are you sure about that?*

"I don't think I said anything funny."

She thought a moment trying to figure out how to word what she wanted to say to him. She didn't want him to pretend this to be something it wasn't. The lines were already a little blurry for her. Nico turned out to be so much more than she ever thought he would and so far she liked everything she discovered about him. That scared her. She didn't want to start thinking they had a relationship when she knew they didn't. Not a real one at least. "I'm not different, Nico. I'm a fling. I know what you want and I'm okay with that."

The pad of his thumb started caressing circles on her stomach. The movement felt so intimate. Especially when he dropped feather kisses on the back of her neck. God the man made her feel good. Not just sexually either. He made her feel good about herself. Made her smile, laugh.

"What if I'm not?" He whispered in a husky, sultry tone against her neck.

"What if you're not what?"

"Okay with this being a fling?"

Warmth spread through her body at the same time confusion slammed her head. He couldn't be saying what it sounded like. Nico suddenly wanting a relationship didn't make sense. It didn't fit who he was. "You aren't looking for a relationship. We want different things. You've said so and so have I." The words didn't want to pass her lips. Why she didn't know. She wasn't in love with him. Sure she cared about him, liked him, enjoyed his company but she wasn't in love with him. She'd felt love before and knew how it felt when the emotion bloomed. *Didn't she?* Right now she wasn't so sure.

"I wasn't looking for a relationship but one found me all the same, *Tesoro*. I'm not ready to release whatever hold you have somehow put on me." His hand moved up and cupped one breast. "You've bewitched me. Cast a spell on me. I can't make you any promises, Tabby." His thumb rubbed her nipple sending shocks of delight through her body. "I don't know how good I'll be at this whole relationship thing but I want to give it a try. With you.

"I know I'm not exactly what you're looking for but we're good together." His voice whispered a seductive song to her soul. "I want to be yours. To call you mine. To bust assholes like Lance in the face when they look at you the way he did the other night."

She knew what it sounded like he was saying but she had to be sure. She never expected this from this confirmed bachelor. Tabby rolled over. Their faces only a couple inches apart. "What exactly are you saying, Nico?"

"Live a little. Give me a chance. Let's see where this can take us."

She never expected this. Her mind struggled to understand how they'd gotten here. Nico flirted, not only with her but with women in general. She wanted that one special person who would make her number one in their lives. Someone who she could do the same with, someone who she could have a forever kind of bond with. The two just didn't mix. Or they didn't until she met him

Nico treated her like she was someone special to him, someone he cared about, and obviously someone he wanted to attempt a relationship with which happened to be a first for him. That made her special, didn't it? As much as she tried to prevent it he'd become someone special to her. He meant more to her than anyone in a long time. Nico was worth the risk. She just had to keep reminding herself he wasn't making promises. They could take it one step at a time.

He leaned forward lightly touching his lips to hers before pulling away. The kiss was sweet, sensual, melting what little resistance she had left. *Please don't let this be a mistake.* "So we're going to give this a shot? Officially date? With titles and everything?"

"Now don't start trying to scare me." Nico laughed.

She could see a playful twinkle dance in his eyes. She loved that about him. He could always make her smile, make a heavy moment light with just a few words. "You try changing your mind now and I won't be responsible for my actions." Tabby playfully made a fist and waved it in front of him. "You're stuck with me." For how long, she didn't know. A leopard couldn't change his spots. He might decide this isn't what he really wanted, she might discover he couldn't give her what she needed but for the first time in a long time she felt hopeful. The emotion filled her up. He made her happier than anyone she'd ever known.

"Are you kidding, Slugger? I've been on the receiving end of your right hook before. You're one scary chick."

She tried to think of a smart aleck reply but before she could Nico rolled on top of her and kissed her. His tongue plunged into her mouth treating her to his addictive taste. He kissed her senseless, kissed all thoughts besides him out of her head. She knew she'd wanted to say something but at the moment she had no idea what it had been.

Chapter Ten

Tabby rolled over to hug Nico but she was alone. He'd thoroughly ravaged her last night. So much so that she slept so soundly she obviously didn't hear him leave. She felt a little bummed that he left without saying goodbye. Trying not to think negative she decided something came up, he probably had plans and didn't want to wake her. *Or maybe he had second thoughts and doesn't want to hurt me.* She pushed those negative thoughts from her head. If he changed his mind then she'd deal with it. No more broken hearts for her. No more crying over men.

After a good stretch Tabby stood up and padded toward her bathroom naked. As soon as she turned the corner into her hallway she bumped into a bare chested, sexy as sin, Nico. His hair was a rumpled mess, nothing new there. He had on his jeans, the button undone and nothing else. On auto pilot Tabby ran her finger under her lip to make sure there was no drool. He looked that good.

"I was just coming to wake you."

"Why? What's up?" A nervous quiver shook her voice. She tried to hide it to no avail. She didn't want him to know how strongly he affected her body responses.

"You need to pack a bag. We're going to Half Moon Bay for the night."

Trying to sound as light and carefree as he did she said, "A romantic night away? Are you sure you haven't done this whole relationship thing before?"

He bent and captured her mouth in a kiss, his lips seductively caressing hers to open. He tasted of mint and man. Tabby placed her hands on the smooth skin of his chest. His sinewy body sizzled with intense heat. Unable to hold back Tabby let her hands roam his body, not just his chest but his back as well. After an all too short exploration Nico pulled away.

"We better stop or we'll never get out of here."

She wasn't so sure that was a bad thing but then she remembered where they were going. If he planned to take her away for the night there would be time later to burn up the sheets with him. Anticipation raced through her body. She couldn't wait to find out what he had in store for her. What she knew about Nico told her it would be like nothing she'd ever experienced before. Everything they did together felt unique. He made even the smallest of things fresh, new. When they got to Half Moon Bay she'd have to be sure and show him just how much she appreciated him.

For the first time in his life nerves ticked inside his body over a woman. Today needed to be special. He wanted her to know how much she meant to him. He needed to try and prove to her and himself that he could handle this whole relationship thing. "You're not afraid of heights are you?" Glancing quickly her way he saw her head shake no before he turned to face the freeway once again. They'd taken her car. She had one but rarely drove it in the city. Traffic made it much easier to take cabs in downtown San Francisco.

"Why?"

"Have you ever taken a helicopter ride?"

"No way?" Excitement laced her response making the blood in his own veins pump faster.

"Yep, Slugger, what did you think we'd do, go to dinner and the movies? Not on my watch, baby." For some strange reason he wanted to impress her. He wanted her to know he would do whatever it took to make her happy and show her a good time. "In just a few minutes we'll be boarding a helicopter and taking a tour of the Bay area. I did this tour with Gabriella a couple years back. The city looks totally different when you're looking down on it."

"Ah, so this is how you show all the girls a good time?"

She had a small smile on her face probably meant to make her words sound playful but the small tug on her lips didn't fool him. "No Slugger, this isn't how I show all the girls a good time. Gabriella is my sister. She won it on some radio contest."

"I shouldn't have asked that."

"No biggie. I don't have anything to hide, Tabby. You asked a legitimate question. We both know how things used to be for me. There's no reason to shy away from the truth. But no matter what I've done, or who I've dated I want you to know that I'm with you and only you right now." He wanted a future with her so he wouldn't hide his past, not that he could anyway. Of all things he wanted her to know the first was he'd always be upfront with her. If they wanted to give this a real go she had to know that his past was his past, his future was a different story. He couldn't change who he was and despite what people may think his actions meant, of all things he was honest and loyal.

He glanced at her again to see her eyes locked on him. Damn she had to be the most beautiful woman he'd ever seen. He hated sounding like a sap but she mesmerized him. He'd take a lot of shit if people knew how big a softie she turned him into. The Pillsbury dough boy had nothing on what Tabby did to him. You've finally lost it, he thought to himself but when Tabby reached out and stroked his leg damned if he cared.

"So how many sisters do you have?" She needed to lighten the mood. Their brief but intense eye contact made her start thinking all sorts of things she knew she shouldn't. Not this soon. They'd just decided to officially be a couple. Who knew how soon it would be before Nico tired of the monogamy. He usually had a different woman every week. Would he be able to handle being exclusive?

"Three. I'm sure you've met Maria. She helps Kaylee out at her store when she's not in school. She's nineteen. Theresa is twenty one, and Gabriella's twenty four. They're great girls. I can't wait for you to meet them."

He surprised her with his words. Did he plan to bring her home to meet his family? She couldn't do the same. She had no family to bring him home to. She'd never had that but she wanted it. Tabby envied him that. Nico loved his family. Pride and love ignited in his words. She knew they felt the same about him. Who wouldn't? "I'm sure they are great. I bet you chased off any guy that ever looked their way."

"Hell yes. I know exactly how a man thinks and anyone who dares think it about my little sisters will have me to deal with."

He spoke with a smile on his face and laughter in his eyes but she knew part of him to be serious. Nico would protect people he cared about. He proved that with the way he pushed Luciano toward Kaylee. He wanted his cousin to be happy and he did everything he could to make it happen. "Big tough guy, huh? Afraid they'll bring home a guy like you?"

"Hey. What's wrong with me? I'm a damn gentleman. Here I am taking my woman on a surprise helicopter ride and a night at a bed and breakfast. I think I deserve a reward when we're alone tonight."

Her heart did a summersault in her chest. He called her his woman and damned if it didn't tickle her insides. She suddenly felt hot, like she was glued to the leather upholstery of her car seat. And she wanted to give him something special for what she knew would be one of the best days of her life. They hadn't done any of the things he planned yet and it already was. "You have yourself deal, Nico. I have a sexy surprise in store for you." When she heard him let out a groan she continued, "You know before I met you I wasn't what you'd call, frisky. A couple nights with you and all that's changed."

Tabby buckled her seatbelt and put her headset on. Her limbs shook slightly whether from nerves or excitement she couldn't tell. Both emotions flowed through her body as the helicopter lifted off the ground. A fluttering began to stir in her belly as they lifted higher. Nico grabbed her hand and squeezed. The gesture was so simple but yet so meaningful. It added an increased heart rate along with everything else she felt.

"You okay, Slugger?"

Oh yeah. Better than okay. As they lifted and the pilot's voice flowed through the earpiece she knew they were setting out on an adventure. A once in a lifetime kind of thing. Not that she could never do this again but it would be different. Today was a surprise, an idea that he had to make her day special, to make her feel special and that meant more to her than she could tell him. "Perfect." On instinct Tabby leaned forward and placed a simple kiss on his lips.

Nico moved his arm around her and pulled her toward him so she could look out his window. He winked at her before turning toward the scenery that passed them. They passed over Bay Meadows Horse track, The Port of San Francisco, and the Bay Bridge before they headed over Alcatraz Island. Growing up here she'd seen in all before but not like this. The view couldn't be more amazing, looking down at beautiful San Francisco landmarks, calming music floating through her headset, Nico holding her tight. Amazing.

Her stomach felt fluttery, like the wings of butterflies tickled inside her. She'd never forget this day. A content calmness bathed her. For the first time she didn't feel like she had to prove herself, she didn't need to look for anything or anyone to make her happy because right now she had everything she needed. A friend who cared about her, someone who meant more to her each day they spent together, respect, happiness.

She had so much, a job she loved, two girlfriends who meant the world to her, yet she'd always wanted more. She wanted that unconditional, in sickness and health, knight in shining armor kind of love and she never thought she'd rest until she had it. Looking over the Pacific Ocean stretching beyond view she realized how insignificant her expectations really were. That perfect man didn't exist. But the man sitting next to her was pretty darn close.

She knew they had to take this one step at a time. Life threw curve balls but whatever happened she'd always be grateful for this time. She had everything she ever wanted within grasp. Too bad it took her so long to figure it out.

Nico tapped her shoulder shaking her free of the thoughts that grasped her mind. "Look, *Tesoro*." He pointed towards the water at Montera Beach. "Do you see the whale?"

The beautiful, majestic humpback whale lowered in the water before floating to the surface again. It rolled over before disappearing beneath the blue water below them. "Wow." All other words escaped her.

The helicopter began to turn. She leaned into Nico burying her face in his neck. "Thank you." He kissed her forehead as the helicopter soared back to their take-off point. The simple kiss was more intimate than anything she'd experienced with him so far.

After their tour ended they drove into Half Moon Bay and ate at a small Italian Bistro with a cobblestone walkway and a patio decorated with tables and umbrellas. They both ordered cheese ravioli with pesto. When Tabby mentioned how much she loved pesto Nico bragged about his secret recipe that according to him made it even more mouth-watering.

"Well you're supposed to be giving me cooking lessons," she told him. "Next time I expect to learn your secret pesto ingredient." Tabby scooped the last bite on her plate and ate it.

"I don't know about that, Slugger. You're going to have to convince me. I don't share my secret recipes with just anyone." He leaned back in the chair a devilish grin on his face.

"What do I have to do to convince you?" She played along.

His grin turned into a seductive weapon that her body proved to be helpless against. She melted on the spot as her nipples puckered wanting the attention of his mouth.

"I'm sure you'll figure something out, Slugger."

They pulled into the parking lot of The Landis Shore's Oceanfront Inn a beautiful bed and breakfast sitting right on the ocean. Her body began to betray her as nervous energy jolted through her body. This day meant so much to her, he treated her like she meant so much to him. Almost like...no, no way could she let herself start thinking like that. Thoughts of love always ended in pain for her. She refused to let that happen. Not this time.

A few minutes later they entered The Tuscany Room. It was perfect. Coffee brown and sand tones decorated the room accented with coral to complete the Italian, yet the-ocean-is-right-outside-my-door look the room encompassed. Tabby dropped her bag right inside the doorway, unable to keep herself from exploring all the room had to offer. The floors were an Italian stone, travertine which she'd used herself decorating in the past. Tabby stepped into the bathroom to find a whirlpool tub with granite surrounding it that brought back all sorts of memories of how they'd spent the night before.

Breaking free of the memory she stepped past the queen size bed to stand in front of a sliding glass door which lead to a private balcony overlooking the Pacific. She couldn't help but stare at the view, her eyes lost, soaking in the beautiful surroundings while her mind never strayed from the man now standing directly behind her, his hands on her shoulders. She felt an electric charge shoot through her body at the contact.

"Do you like it?" Nico kissed her neck, his hands gently massaging her shoulders.

"Yes."

"Who'd have thought a player like me had it in him to be

sweet and romantic? I knew you'd be surprised." His words weren't meant to be taken seriously. Just a joke, something he loved to do but still Tabby felt guilty. She hadn't given Nico the credit he deserved. She'd seen him as a ladies' man who never took women seriously, which couldn't be farther from the truth. He may have dated a lot but she had no doubt that he treated all women with respect.

"I've been a bitch to you. I don't know why you didn't give up a long time ago." She turned to face him wrapping her arms around his waist. "I never gave you the benefit of the doubt. I saw you as a flirtatious heartbreaker who had string of women trailing behind him. I'm sorry about that."

He looked a little taken-back by her words. Like he hadn't expected them, or maybe even like he was a little confused by what she told him.

"Well I had my reputation to protect so I didn't wear my sweet and caring hat too often in public." He offered a wink. "I wouldn't want it getting out that when the right lady comes a long I turn into a chick-flick sap."

The right woman? Oh God was this really starting to turn into something? Trying not to over think his comment Tabby tried to follow his light mood by swatting his behind. "I'm being serious, Nico. I really am sorry."

"There's nothing to be sorry about, Slugger. Except for the slap, I'm never going to let you live that one down."

She still had her arms around him as they rocked back and forth looking at each other. "Agh, I hate that I did that."

"I think you like to get a little rough. So far you've smacked me, and just now you swatted my ass. You know, I like a little spanking as long as I'm the one giving it."

How could he do that? Sound seductive, playful and sensual all at the same time? Instantly making her wet for him. The man had skills. "Are you going to take this conversation seriously and just accept my apology?"

"Nope. I want to get back to talking about spanking." He pulled her closer. Her breasts flattened against the hard wall of his chest.

"Fine I guess I'll have to add that to the list of things I have to make up to you, convince you of, or thank you for." And she knew just how to do it. Tabby dropped to her knees not caring that they stood in front of a glass door that faced the beach. She ran her hand up and down the bulge in Nico's pants before she unbuttoned and unzipped them. When she reached in and pulled his massively hard erection free she heard a faint mutter above her of, "Holy shit."

Nico's whole body trembled. Countless women had gone down on him in the past, yet he trembled like this was the first time. And the sad part was she didn't even have her mouth on him yet. Damn this woman had some kind of hold on him. She was like a magician. She had some invisible grasp on him that tightened every time he saw her or even talked to her. When he felt her ease his clothes down his legs he almost lost it. Her smooth finger traced a path down his legs as she went.

His last logical thought before she licked a path down his cock was to reach out and close the blinds on the glass door. This moment belonged to them. He wouldn't share it with anyone. Then it came, the hot lick of her tongue around the head of his erection. Nico moved his hand to her hair, running his fingers through her cropped black hair, the silky strands wrapping around his fingers.

His whole body burned with sizzling hot desire as Tabby took him in her warm, wet mouth. Heaven. That's the only word he could think of to describe this feeling. Looking down he almost lost his balance watching her luscious mouth taking as much of him in as she could. "So beautiful. That feels so good, Tesoro." She peaked up at him, her eyes smiling, telling him she enjoyed giving him this pleasure. He held back from coming right there. Hell no would he let them end this soon.

A second later she added her hand to the mix. Her hand and mouth worked him at the same time. Damn he'd never felt something so good, so hot as Tabby's mouth on him. White hot need shot through his body moving his arms to pull her up so she stood face to face with him. "You feel so good, baby. If I don't stop you now we'd be over before we had the chance to begin."

Grabbing the bottom of her shirt, he pulled it up and over her head. He ran his hand across her flat belly, around her waist and up her back. She had the most amazing skin, silky, smooth like the best fine chocolate. Her lavender scent filled the air around them. So sweet, so feminine, everything about her turned him on, made his chest feel a strange sort of tightness that felt completely foreign to him. His hands couldn't stop taking her in, feeling every part of her torso like they'd never touched before.

She began to do the same, her fingers exploring him under his shirt with expert skill. Hell, anything she did to him felt perfect. Nico stopped his hands from their journey long enough for her to pull his shirt over his head, then he touched her again, pulling her tight against him for a searing hot kiss. Unable to hold back he plunged his tongue in her mouth while he unhooked her bra. Two simple flicks of his fingers and her bra fell to the floor.

"You are way too good at that," she whispered against his mouth.

He grabbed her ass and lifted her so that her legs wrapped around him. Damn, he'd wanted to do this for so long. "I'm a sexpert. What can I say?" Tabby burst into uncontrollable laughter. Her warm breath against his face, her gorgeous smile making him get even harder than he already was.

"That was so bad, Nico. A sexpert? I mean, I'm not arguing with you or anything but you just laid the cheese on pretty thick."

He held her tight, watching her, seeing her happiness, his own happiness reflecting in her eyes. He loved this side of her. This fun, silly side that she began to show around him more and more. "You're the only woman who's ever called me cheesy, Slugger." Nico laid her on the bed and looked down at her. "Sexy, funny, the best damn lay in the whole world, now those I've heard before. Cheesy, not so much." Lowering his mouth, he sucked a pert, brown nipple into his mouth.

"How about conceited. Anyone ever call you that?"

She sounded more breathless than before. More turned on. Flicking her nipple with his tongue he said, "Not conceited, *Tesoro*, just honest." He sucked and licked before switching to her other breast. He needed to taste them equally. Every part of her body tasted so damn good to him.

"You're very good at that."

He felt her hands start winding through his hair. Hell yeah. He liked her like this. Turned on and sexy as hell. "You're very good too, Tabby. The best. I could feel your hands on me every hour of every day and never tire of it."

She didn't reply. Just continued to run one hand through his hair while the other traced a path up and down his back. With one hand Nico undid the button and zipper on her pants and eased a hand in, dipped below her panties until he felt her wet heat. "Mm, baby, you're so wet for me."

"Yes."

Two fingers sank inside her. Her velvety softness clamped around them. He started to work in and out, feeling her grasp his fingers like a glove as he went. God he could be here forever, tasting her breasts, feeling the warmth of her body on his hand, and soon his cock. Responding to the movements of her body Nico increased the pace. She gasped every now and again, little moans escaped her, her hand tightened in his hair. Her body was a firecracker. When he was ready to feel her come he lit the match, rubbing his thumb on her clitoris while nibbling at her breast.

She tightened around him, tensed, called his name, and then fell back limp against the bed.

Dear God this man could give orgasms like nobody's business. When he said he knew women he didn't lie. Inside and out Nico knew how to give to a woman. Sexually and every other way as well. That's why she'd gone down on him earlier. She wanted to give back to him as well. He had no way of knowing how much he'd given her in the past couple weeks. "Damn boy, you know what you're doing."

His rich laughter filled the room. "See what you'd been missing all these months? We have a lot of time to make up for. I'm nowhere near finished with you yet."

Tabby followed Nico with her eyes as he stood up and walked naked to the small fridge in the room. The man had a fine body. Long, lean, golden, and strong. He walked with an air of confidence. Not arrogant or conceited, but confident, he knew who he was and what he wanted. She loved that about him. *Loved? Wow, slow down girl. Where did that come from?* Falling in love with him wouldn't be smart. She better curb that thought now.

Nico sauntered back toward the bed, strawberries, chocolate, and whipped cream in hand. Oh boy. Things were starting to get sticky, in more ways than one. He set the food on the bed before hooking his fingers in her pants and pulling them down her legs.

"I'm a chef and I love food, baby." He looked her in the eyes. Probably noticing the apprehension she figured reflected there. "Did you really think an Italian Chef wouldn't incorporate food with sex?" He dropped her clothes to the floor. "Damn you're beautiful, Tabby. Two of my favorite things." He opened the whipped cream and put a dab on each of her nipples. Warmth spread through her body contrasting the cold cream. He bent and licked the whipped cream off one breast then the other. "Food and you. Damn I'm a lucky man."

She shivered. Her toes curled. Her whole body burst with anticipation. He smelled sexy, manly, looked eager and ready to please. No happy to please, like he wanted nothing more than for them to take pleasure from one another. Give and take.

"Hungry?" He put a strawberry to her lips. Tabby took a bite, the juice dripping down her chin.

She reached up to wipe it off but Nico grabbed her hand before she could. "I'm getting that." He did. With his tongue.

Unexpected Mr. Right   **141**

Licking the sweet juice off her, she heard him moan before he captured her mouth, kissing her like there was no tomorrow. The succulent juice of the strawberry lingered on his tongue and mixed with Nico's unique taste to create a flavor she could quickly become addicted to. Hell, just the man himself was enough to addict her.

Nico pulled away to feed her another bite. He dropped more whipped cream on her breasts, a dab of chocolate and began to feast on her. A mix of sensations exploded throughout her body, the coolness of the cream, the warmth of his tongue, the fire of her desire for him.

"Mm, *Tesoro*. You taste so good, feel so good."

Nico moved so every inch of his hard body straddled hers. His cock nestled the apex of her thighs making her hips lunge forward of their own accord. She felt a hot path burn from her breast to her neck as he began to nuzzle her neck.

"God, Nico you feel good. I need you inside of me. All of you."

His teeth nipped at her neck before he grabbed a condom and sheathed himself. He entered her swiftly, burying himself to the hilt, filling her up in the most pleasureful way.

"This is more than just sex, *Tesoro*." He said the words softly, then he started to move in the most delicious way. Tabby ran her hand across his back, feeling his muscles constrict as he pushed in and out of her. Oh yeah, this was more than sex. Fear gripped her at where it headed for her. What she started to feel. No, not right now. All she wanted to think about now is the pleasure that possessed her body.

Nico kissed her deeply as he thrust inside her, stretched her in the most wonderful way. She matched the rhythm he set, meeting him thrust for delicious thrust. "So close," she whispered against his mouth. He didn't kiss her again, just watched her until the intimacy became too much. Her eyes drifted closed, her body still moving with his.

"Look at me."

He issued it like a command. She couldn't deny him so she did as he said, kept eye contact while they moved together.

Out of her peripherals she saw his strong arms hold him up, one on each side of her head making her feel engulfed by him.

"Come for me, Tabby. I can feel you tighten, your body getting wetter. You're ready. Let go."

His voice did her in. She let loose and climaxed, her body soaring, exploding with bliss. His release followed right behind her, he groaned before collapsing on top of her. His weight made it hard to breathe but she didn't care. Having Nico this close felt too damn good to ask him to move.

Chapter Eleven

Nico lay in bed watching Tabby stand on the balcony, a plush robe covering her, binoculars held to her face looking out at the ocean. Her sexy curves beckoned him. Even with the robe covering her she looked sexy as hell, curvy, feminine and his. And this time he meant the forever kind. She didn't know it yet. He couldn't believe it himself but he knew it, felt it deep to the marrow of his bones.

After they made love another time he'd held her, fed her strawberries and talked to her. The conversation was light, about their day, her work, Luciano and Kaylee's wedding but it felt like so much more just because it came from her mouth. He studied her face, the way her eyes lit when she spoke about the wedding, the way she frowned when a topic she didn't like came up, the small dimple under the left side of her mouth when she smiled. Everything about her turned him on. Even more than that it touched his heart.

Strange but true. The man who never planned to fall in love had gone and done that very thing. And with a woman who he didn't know if she did or would ever feel the same way about him. She had these standards in her head that she thought she had to have. The why of it he didn't know but he sure as hell planned to find out. No way could he let her know how he felt until he did.

Nico wanted to laugh. Who would have thought he'd be

sitting in bed contemplating how to win a woman over? How to get her to see him as the forever kind of man? Sure as hell not him. Not anyone else he knew. Especially not her. The funniest part is he wasn't scared. Not in the least. Of all the women he'd ever known, ever been with, no one got to him like she did. That told him something right there and he wasn't one to argue.

Suddenly getting tied down didn't sound like the crazy as hell concept he'd always thought it to be. Hell, he'd have a woman he could flirt with, pamper, and laugh with any time he wanted. Just like his parents. As long as he could make her believe him, make her that he was Mr. Right. The concept still amazed him. He wanted to be her Mr. Right. He might not be the prince charming kind of man she always thought she'd end up with but they belonged together. He wanted her and he would have her. He knew women. He'd find a way to make her see she finally found the one.

The next morning Tabby woke up in Nico's arms. The whole thing felt surreal. She was dating a man she never thought she would. A guy who wanted different things than her. This should feel wrong but for some reason it didn't. She felt more right than she had in a long time. Happy. Happy where she was in her life, not looking for something more than she had right now. Content.

After she finished site-seeing on the balcony last night, they'd showered together, made love again, then watched a movie in bed before falling asleep. They were comfortable together. Almost like an old married couple who'd done the same thing together every night for years. She liked it. She liked him. Maybe too much.

Nico had their breakfast served in their room. They ate on the balcony, talking before dressing and getting on the road to head home. He had to work tonight. She wanted to get a few things done as well. Time to leave their utopia and step back

Unexpected Mr. Right   **145**

into reality. "What do you have planned this week?"

"I work a few nights and have to help Luciano with some last minute wedding plans." He glanced at her veering onto the off-ramp. "Remember Friday Luciano's is closed for that pre-wedding dinner or whatever it is."

"Yeah, I remember. I can't believe their wedding is almost here. I'm so happy for her."

"I'm happy for both of them. I wasn't sure Luciano would ever walk down the aisle. Too much to risk. That whole ball and chain thing is scary for some men."

A twinge of shock sparked inside her. Why, she didn't know. She'd always known Nico never wanted to settle down. Did she think after the amazing weekend they spent together he would suddenly change his mind? Not likely. Just because he wanted them to be in a "relationship" didn't mean he would ever want the things she did. Confirmed bachelors rarely changed. And if they did she wondered how many of those relationships actually worked out?

Probably not very many. His words, though playful, reminded her to keep her heart closed. She couldn't risk handing it over to him. Not when she wasn't sure he wanted it. The pain would crush her. More than anyone had hurt her before.

"Well I'm glad they both came to their senses and realized how perfect they could be together." Her words were meant to sound light. Letting him know what really went on in her head scared her. Hell, it would probably scare him even more. Luckily they pulled up at her apartment so she could make her escape.

"I know you have stuff you need to do and so do I so I'll just head in and let you get going. Thanks for a great weekend, Nico." She kissed him swiftly, trying to be nonchalant, like his words didn't hurt her because she knew they shouldn't. He'd never lied to her. Hell, his words weren't even directed at them but at Luciano and Kaylee so why did she let it affect her so much? *Because you're falling in love with him. He's starting to mean too much to you.*

Tabby grabbed for the handle but Nico stopped her. "What's wrong, Slugger?"

"Nothing." The reply slipped out of her mouth automatically even though it was a lie.

"Why are you trying to make a quick escape then?" His eyes pierced her like he could see straight down to her soul.

"I'm not."

"Well then, how do you explain trying to jump out of your own car? You're stuck with me for at least a few more minutes. Whether you like it or not I'm coming up at least while I wait for a cab. Unless after the weekend we just had together you're going to make a poor guy walk home."

Smooth move, Tab. "I think I'm a little tired from last night. My mind is playing tricks on me." They locked her car and headed to her apartment.

"I think the night we had makes a little bit of memory lapse worth it. You were quite the wanton."

"Don't let it go to your head there big guy." Teasing him made her smile, made the inside of her tummy feel achy. She enjoyed him so much. Everything about him. All the things she didn't think she'd like, the playfulness, the flirtatiousness. But then he did have a serious side too. One she saw more the closer they became. Seconds ago she'd been feeling down. He made her forget that quickly. Scary thought. This wasn't the time to lose her head.

"Why shouldn't I? Weren't you the one who said you weren't what was the word? Oh yeah, frisky. I think you're very frisky." He moved toward her to give her a kiss. The phone rang giving her the perfect excuse to back up. She needed space right now. The intense weekend they had, coupled with their conversation in the car had her feeling like a ball of jumbled emotions. She needed to get things figured out.

"It's your cab," she said glancing down at caller ID. She

quickly picked up the phone and told the driver he'd be right down. Unable to hold herself back Tabby gave him a soft fleeting kiss on the lips before opening the door for him. "Thanks for a great weekend, Nico."

Five days had passed and she still hardly talked to him. First he thought he'd been imagining things, then he'd been confused, now he was just plain pissed. How could he think he knew women so well? Hell from what he'd witnessed the past few weeks, women didn't even know what they wanted so how could he? Nico dropped a box of wine bottles on a table. "I don't want to go out with you Nico," he said in a mocking female voice. "Oh, maybe we can just be friends. Well, I guess we can be friends with benefits."

Roughly he pulled bottles from the box and set them on the table. "No wait, I agree with you, lets' try to be in a committed relationship. Never mind, I think I'll give you the cold shoulder all week."

"Why are you talking like a woman, Nico?"

"Jesus." Nico jumped at the sound of Luciano's voice. He ran his hand though his hair trying not to smile at how crazy he'd probably sounded. "Make a little bit of noise when you come in next time can you? A little warning would be nice so I can save face by not stalking around talking to myself in my girly man voice." Pulling out a chair Nico sat down.

"Be right back. Looks like the conversation calls for a little bit of alcohol." Luciano poured them each a shot of Tequila and sat down at the table.

"What's wrong?"

"Tabby has my balls, that's what's wrong." Nico downed his shot.

"That wouldn't have you stalking around sounding like you need a pair of heels and a dress. You sure it's not an organ a little farther north?"

Yeah, didn't feel so good on this side of the conversation.

He'd liked it much more when he'd been the one getting Luciano to open up about his feelings. "Naw, that's not it." *It wasn't*. Well at least he didn't think so. This whole situation had him so messed up he didn't know that the hell to think. He felt just as indecisive as her.

Yeah right. That wasn't really the case. He knew deep inside that Luciano was right. No other excuse made and sense. This started out about getting in her bed and now he'd been there. Multiple times. If that's all he wanted from her he'd be on his way by now. He wouldn't be stalking around confused over a woman. New territory for him since he'd become involved with her.

"This is all about sex then? Don't play yourself. That's bullshit and we both know it, cousin."

Aw, hell. Luciano was right. "Yeah, maybe I am starting to care for her. I think I'm falling for her, Lu." The words weren't as hard to get out as he thought they would be. Still, hearing them out loud shocked him to the core. Sorting through the things in his mind, and for the first time in his life a woman had his heart and the shitty part is he wasn't sure she really wanted it. Hell he wasn't sure he deserved to give it to her.

"So what's the problem?"

"She can't seem to make up her mind. First she wanted nothing to do with me, then we could be friends, we eventually moved on to an actual relationship, now I can hardly get two words out of her."

Nico watched Luciano down his shot before he replied. "And it's all her fault? Are you sure you didn't send her any mixed signals along the way? When you got her to forgive you for the whole Cindy incident didn't you tell her you would just be friends?"

"Yeah, so?"

"Think about it Nic, maybe she's been a little confused too. You can't just put this blame on her. I think you've been just as big a part of all the flip-flopping back and forth, don't you?"

Nico glanced up at the chandelier above the table getting lost in the white glow of the lights. *Shit*. Since when did

Luciano get so damn smart? Maybe love did that to a guy, let them see things they didn't before. But then, he wasn't so all knowing all of a sudden and for the first time in his life he was in love with a woman. Must have skipped him.

"See what I'm saying?"

"Yeah but why the silent treatment all of a sudden? We had a blast this weekend then all of a sudden she clammed up on me and we've hardly spoken since." He spun the shot glass on the table, watching it wobble before becoming still again. This whole situation was fucked up. He'd never been so confused by a woman in his life. He didn't like it.

"See that's what you have to learn about women, Nico. There's a reason for everything. We might not know what we did wrong, once we find out we might not even understand how we were wrong, but know this," he cocked a smile. "We're always wrong. We always did something we just have to figure out what the hell is was."

Nico mulled over what his cousin said, trying to wrack his brain for what he did but came up with nothing.

"Does she know how you feel?"

"No."

"Well that's probably part of it right there, Casanova. Tabby's run by her heart. It's in everything she does. I think you two would be great together, Nico, I really do. But you need to be sure. I don't want to see her hurt. If you are, tell her how you feel. She needs to hear it." Luciano stood up and glanced at his watch. "We need to hurry and get things ready around here. Everyone will be here soon. Think about it, Nic, then talk to her."

This sucked. Her palms continued to sweat no matter how many times she wiped them. Her heart beat with quick, pounding thumps in her chest that couldn't be healthy. Tabby couldn't say why she was so nervous but as her cab got closer and closer to Luciano's her symptoms intensified. Tonight would be the first time she'd seen Nico after their fabulous, yet confusing weekend in Half Moon Bay.

She had no idea how to act. He'd called her multiple times but she hadn't said much, tried to keep the conversations short and to the point. She had to keep her emotions in check so she didn't get too close to him. Tonight would be a true test for her. *Test my ass. Torture is more like it.* The fact is, she missed him. She wanted nothing more than to run up to him, hug him and spend hours making love and talking. But she couldn't. She needed to keep her distance. Plus tonight was about Luciano and Kaylee. Their family. Their love. Their upcoming wedding. It had nothing to do with her.

That made her sad. Not that she didn't want Kaylee to have this time. She did. Seeing her friend this happy meant the world to her but still, she couldn't help but wonder, when or if her own time would ever come. She'd forgotten about it for a while but with the wedding fast approaching, and her new found, completely stupid feelings for Nico all her wishes started to resurface. Big mistake.

The cab pulled up against the curb in front of Luciano's. The sign read closed but she knew inside would be a whole clan of Valenti's, Kaylee, her mom and new step dad, and friends and family of both the bride and the groom. Most of all she knew Nico stood inside the building. She could feel him, knew he stood by the window looking out at her probably wondering why the hell she'd turned into a bitch again. She hated that. Didn't want him to see her that way but she couldn't help but put the defense mechanism in place to guard her heart.

After paying her cabbie, she got out of the car, straightened her red flowy skirt, fixed her white silk tank top and headed into the restaurant. She stepped in the door to find Bri standing there looking mad as hell. "What's wrong, girl? You have your scary Bri face on right now."

"I'm just trying to figure out why *that man* is here."

"Who? Sorry I don't understand angry Brianna talk."

Bri gave her the don't go there look. "Jackson. I mean, I know Kaylee invited Mama Love but why the hell did she

Unexpected Mr. Right   151

have to go and invite him? It's already bad enough that I have to see him at home. Now he's barged his way into the rest of my life."

Tabby tried not to smile but to no avail. She'd never seen Bri like this before. She couldn't help but wonder what it meant. "I'm sure Mama Love didn't want to come on her own."

"Hello? What am I? I could have brought her."

"Maybe he wanted to come so he could make sure she's safe. He's probably still worried about her since the mugging."

"I doubt that. I don't think the man has a heart."

Hm, this is interesting. If she didn't know better Tabby would think Bri liked him. That is if it was anyone but Brianna they were talking about. When she liked someone she wasn't afraid to admit it. She'd approach him, have her way with him, then kick him to the curb. "I guess he just came to make your life a living hell then. Maybe he's stalking you."

"Ha, ha very funny. Looks like Nico's rubbing off on you. You're finally loosening up a bit."

Tabby smacked her in the arm with her purse. "Hey. I've always been loose." With one look from Bri she realized what she just said. "Oh, shut up. You know what I mean." They both laughed and finished walking into the restaurant. God she was lucky. She had the best friends. Without them she'd be completely alone. Bri and Kaylee could always make her smile, help ease her tension with a joke and a smile. *Kind of like Nico.*

"Great. He's coming this way." Brianna squeezed her arm as Tabby looked up to see Jackson coming their way.

"I just wanted to apologize if I hurt you the other day," he said to her. "I was a little side tracked with McGruff over there," he pointed to Bri, "and I know I shook you pretty hard."

"Don't call me a dog." Brianna said.

"I didn't. I called you McGruff. I was referring to your crime stopping abilities, not what you are." He crossed his arms. Wow. All sorts of tension flowed between these two and something told Tabby some of it was of the sexual kind. "Don't worry about it. You didn't hurt me. Not that we didn't deserve it for the way we jumped on you."

He gave her a slight nod. "You were just trying to defend your friend. She's the one that went crazy for no reason."

"No reason?" Bri said a little too loudly. "I thought you were trying to break into Mama Love's house."

"I told you I'm her son. You're the one who didn't listen."

"Like anyone would believe a hoodlum trying to jimmy a little old woman's window open."

Tabby just stood there watching the scene unfold between the two of them.

Jackson let out a deep breath obviously realizing the two wouldn't come to any agreements. He turned to her. "I just wanted to apologize. I'm going to find my mother."

"Good riddance," Bri said as he walked way. Then she turned to Tabby. "Can you believe that guy? What a jerk."

"Well we did attack him in his mother's front yard. He has a reason to be a little bit angry."

"Please, the guy is some kind of cop. If he can't handle two women then that's his problem.

Tabby almost told her he'd handled the two of them just fine but she had a feeling Bri wouldn't hear her anyway. For some reason she seemed determined not to like Jackson and once Bri set her mind to something there wasn't any changing it. "Whatever. I just don't want a scene."

"At least he's leaving. Now I might finally enjoy myself at this little shin dig. Where's your man?"

"I don't know. We haven't talked much the past few days."

"So you admit he's your man?"

Oops. She'd fallen right into that trap. Before she could reply Bri spoke again. "Why haven't you talked?"

"I don't want to talk about it." Tabby tried to slip away.

Bri grabbed her arm to stop her then eyed the other side of the room. "Don't look now but Super Chef is right over there. He's giving you the sexiest, I-want-to-devour-every-inch-of-your-hot-body look."

Tabby chanced a quick glance at him and he was indeed looking at her. His soot black lashes and dark brown eyes

Unexpected Mr. Right   **153**

began to penetrate her defenses.

"Oh, no. No, no, no. I can see that look in your eyes. Stop over-thinking this. Go with the flow, Tab. That boy wants you. Hell that look tells me he's halfway in love with you."

Her heart sped up, the blood rushed through her veins in excitement. God, she wanted him. She could so easily fall in love with him. Probably already had but she didn't want to admit it. He'd never want what she did. In the end, they wouldn't be able to give each other what the other needed.

"He's not in love with me, Bri. It's lust plain and simple."

"Well whatever that look is, it's hotter than hell. I say you go over there and let him work out some of the lust with you."

She smiled at her friend. "You're so bad, Bri." But she knew she couldn't avoid him all night. Making a quick decision Tabby said, "I am going to go talk to him. Not to work out the lust but just because I've kind of avoided him this week. He doesn't deserve that."

Tabby started to walk toward him. It was like the crowd parted to give her a clear path to him. He watched her every step of the way leaning against the wall relaxed, his hair a mess, his body covered by black pants and an untucked, button up, black silk shirt. Can you say yum? She sure could. This man did it for her like no other. "Hey," she said when she reached him.

"Hey yourself." His voice dripped with sensuality.

"Sorry we haven't talked very much this week." God that sounded dumb. She really should have thought about what to say before she walked over here.

"You mean sorry you haven't talked to me very much this week. I've tried. Can't very well hold a conversation with myself, Slugger."

He sounded angry and to her surprise maybe a little bit hurt too. Damn, he'd been nothing but nice to her and she repaid him cutting his calls short or avoiding him all together? Not cool. "Sorry, Nico. I—"

She was cut short when Nico pulled her close to him. He smelled so good, so incredibly masculine. His hard body pressed against hers as he dipped his mouth close to her ear. "We'll finish this later. You're not off the hook but we have company."

Tabby turned, as older Italian couple approached, and by the looks of them she knew they were his parents. To their side stood three women. One she recognized as Maria. The other two had to be his other sisters. How could she avoid this meeting? Sure she and Nico had said they were dating but that's before she pulled her disappearing act on him. Plus, she doubted he wanted to do the whole introduce her to his family thing. "I'll go so you can talk with your family." Tabby tried to pull away but Nico held her in place.

"I don't think so, *Tesoro*. I'm not letting you out of my sight tonight."

Nico leaned in and kissed his mom, dad, and three sisters on the cheek. "Hi, Mama, Papa. This is my girlfriend, Tabby."

Chapter Twelve

Oh. My. God. She didn't know how she stood here alive because her heart had stopped beating. Not to mention her breath stopped. No matter how hard she tried she couldn't breathe. She could not believe Nico just introduced her to his family as his girlfriend. His mom, who had to be a good four inches shorter than herself beamed up at her before stepping forward and kissing her on the cheek. "Hello, *Cara*." An ear to ear smile graced her face.

His father stepped forward and kissed her as well. His three sisters hugged her, Gabriella and Teresa introducing themselves and Maria told her it was nice to see her again. Everyone in his family was gorgeous. They all shared similar features including Nico's dark hair. After her breath finally found its way back to her Tabby said, "Hi Mr. and Mrs. Valenti. It's so nice to meet you."

His mom waved her hands as she spoke, "We don't need such formalities. I'm Rosa and this is Angelo." She turned toward her son. "Nico, *e molto bella*."

Okay, she recognized the word, *bella* from Luciano. He always called Kaylee bella so she knew it to mean beautiful. Nico clued her in on what Rosa said when he replied, "Yes, Mama. She is beautiful." Heat singed her cheeks. This was so weird. A few months ago she'd never imagine being introduced to Nico's family as his girlfriend. Her mind wouldn't help but wonder if he'd ever done this before. Was it habit for him to introduce women to his family?

"Hey, Nico, can you come here for a minute?" Luciano called from across the room.

He bent and kissed her forehead. "I'll be right back. Pop, come with me." Nico turned to his mom and sisters. "Keep an eye on her for me, ladies. I don't want her disappearing on me." He winked and walked away. And people say women didn't know what they want. Nico had her so backwards she didn't know what to think. He agreed to just friends, then they added the benefits, now a relationship. And nothing could prepare her for being introduced to his family as his girlfriend. That seemed so beyond the scope of reality to her. She couldn't help but remember all the times in the past he'd told her he didn't want a relationship that he never planned to settle down.

How could she believe he'd changed his mind so quickly? Life just didn't work that way. Or did it? Maybe her fear, the knowledge that Nico could hurt her so badly she might not be able to recover blinded her. Oh God, she didn't know what to think.

"So how long have you and Nico been dating?" Maria asked.

Great. How did she answer this one? Well, we started sleeping together first but decided to make it official a little over a week ago. Somehow she didn't think that would make the best impression on his family. "Um, we've been seeing each other for a while now."

"He's never introduced a woman to us before, you know? They're usually not around long enough. He's never been real big on the idea of settling dow—"

"Teresa! You're going to scare her away," Gabriella added.

"I didn't mean it like that. I was trying to say she must be special."

"Didn't come out like that." Maria frowned at her sister.

Rosa said something in Italian and all three girls stopped talking said goodbye to Tabby then left. "Sit down, *Cara*. My

Unexpected Mr. Right   157

legs are getting tired." Tabby sat down with Nico's mom. "My
son likes you."

How much? That's what she really wanted to ask but
instead she said, "I like him too."

"Yes, you do. I can see it in your eyes."

For the second time in the past few minutes she started to
blush. She should feel uncomfortable talking with Nico's mom
about him but she didn't. Something about the woman was
very comforting, caring. She had kind eyes and talked with her
hands. She smiled and Tabby saw more knowledge than she
wanted to share in the Rosa's face. She didn't have to tell her
what she'd tried to deny to herself. She loved him. She knew
it. Rosa knew it. But neither woman admitted it out loud.

"The girls are right, Nico doesn't bring women home. The
look in his eyes tells me you mean a lot to him. You're special.
For some reason he's never liked the idea with settling down
with a woman. He's never used the word girlfriend to me in
his life."

Tabby felt a little nauseous. The look must have shown
because Rosa said, "Don't be scared, *Cara*. If he can embrace
this change in his feelings you can overcome your fears. He
won't hurt you."

Wow, talk about insightful. Rosa read her like a book. Scary
but true. But her words gave her hope. Truth lied behind them.
Maybe not to the extent she thought, only time would tell that
but something about what his mom said gave her strength. She
made Tabby believe in Nico, made her believe in herself. She
might get hurt, hell the odds were she probably would get hurt
but Nico was worth it. She was worth it. How did she ever
expect a chance at her happily ever after if she ran from the
closest prospect she'd ever had? Instinctively she knew
without Nico, no matter where her life went, it would never be
a true happily ever after anyway.

As if she knew Tabby had just been enlightened, Rosa patted
her hand, stood, and kissed her cheek. "It's very nice to meet
you, *Cara*. I'll see you again soon." Rosa smiled then walked
away.

Tabby sat in the corner of Luciano's lost in the sights around her. Kaylee hugged Luciano, looked up at him and laughed, pure happiness in her eyes. Nico stood talking to his dad and sisters, laughing then ruffling his sister's hair like she was a child. Bri stood by Jackson and Mama Love, shooting daggers at him. He must have decided not to leave and Brianna didn't look happy about it.

The aroma of Italy filled the air. Basil, garlic, tomatoes. People chatted, laughed, drank wine. Tabby just watched. Briefly her eyes strayed from Nico but somehow they quickly found their way back to the sinfully sexy man that stole her heart. She had to try and trust him. He could be everything she ever wanted. For her heart, she knew he was the one, she just feared he'd change his mind. Feared he'd realize that he wasn't ready, that he really didn't want to do the whole relationship thing. He'd never wanted one before so she struggled to believe he really wanted one now.

But God she hoped he did. She wanted to believe in him. No way could she turn her back on him. She'd just enjoy the ride, see where this went and most importantly keep her feelings to herself. Last thing she wanted to do was scare him away.

Nico stopped talking to his dad and made eye contact with her. She didn't stand and he didn't walk toward her they just stared. His gaze turned predatory, molten heat simmered off him so strongly it singed her all the way across the room.

She watched him say something to his dad before he stalked toward her. He was a man on a mission. She could see it in his body language, in the way he moved, the look in his eyes. Her body came alive, her heart raced, her nipples puckered. This man not only won her heart but possessed her body with just a look.

"I thought my mom was still with you. If I'd had known you were on your own I wouldn't have stayed away. I'm not letting you get away from me tonight, Slugger."

She couldn't help but smile at him. He made her tingly. Her mind wanted her to run as far away from him as she could but her heart urged her to stay put. After all, she was the first woman he'd introduced to his family, she was the one he asked to have a relationship with, she was the one he took away for the weekend. That had to mean something, didn't it? It couldn't be a game. Well, it could. She'd seen enough of them but Nico wouldn't do that. At least she didn't think he would.

"I'm not going anywhere. I know I've been...distant this week but...I can't talk about this here. Can we do this later? Can you go home with me tonight?"

Nico grabbed her hand and pulled her up. "Let's go."

"Nico, we can't leave yet. We have to stay and have dinner with everyone."

He pulled her close, wrapped his arms around her and kissed her. No tongue, just sensual caress. Nico leaned his forehead against hers. "You're right. But as soon as we can get away, we're out of here. I want you all to myself."

Dinner seemed to take an eternity. No one could stop talking long enough to actually eat, everyone had to make toasts and declare their happiness for Kaylee and Luciano, yada, yada, yada. Normally she loved something like this, loved to talk marriage, listening to everyone's wishes for the happy couple, and last minute wedding details. Today she didn't. All she wanted to do was go home with Nico, spend time with him and make up for her past week of stupidity.

Finally dinner wrapped up and she had the key in the lock to her apartment. As soon as Nico closed the door she kissed him, hard. Her tongue dove into his mouth as she wrapped her arms around his neck. She should have been embarrassed to attack him like this, but she wasn't. She missed his smell, his taste, the feel of his strong hands that he now had moving through her hair. His long, hard body molded to hers. Her hands ravenously thrust through his hair in return before slipping down to the button on his pants.

He laughed against her mouth. So not a good sign.

"Slow down, baby. We have all night."

"What, Mr. Ladies Man can't keep up?" she teased him feeling lighter than she had in years.

"I assure you. I can keep up. But I'm not letting you off the hook that easy." Despite his words he picked her up and carried her to her bedroom. After laying her on the bed Nico climbed on top of her, resting between her thighs. "There, now you can't go anywhere. We need to talk."

"Now? I'd much rather we take our clothes off."

"I thought you said you weren't frisky? I think you're a wanton."

"Are you complaining?" Tabby kissed him again. He returned her kiss before his lips trailed down to the crease of her neck.

"I'm not complaining. God I want you so much too."

"We can talk later, Nico. I need you right now. You probably don't want to hear that but it's true."

He kissed her with unrestrained passion. A full body kiss that she could feel from the tips of her toes to the top of her head. "Don't," he pulled a mere inch away from her mouth, "assume you know what I want, *Tesoro.*" Even though his words were a whisper they had a demanding edge that tempted her to obey. But she couldn't believe him. Not yet.

"So are we getting naked now?"

He laughed a vibrating laugh that rocked her body. "You win but just because I can't deny that luscious body of yours. Afterwards, we talk." Nico sat up and pulled her shirt over her head. Immediately he unhooked the front clasp on her bra. Oh yeah, he wasn't wasting any time. He shimmied down the bed pulling her skirt and panties with. They fell to the floor with a flick of his wrist.

Her body lay on display for him, completely nude while he sat above her clothed. "This doesn't seem fair." Tabby sat up and reached for his shirt but Nico eased her back to the bed.

"Let me look. Every time I see you it's like I'm seeing you for the first time. I'm starved for you but I can't keep my eyes off you at the same time."

Nico took his hand and gently ran his fingers between her

breasts, down her chest and stomach. Her body shivered with delight. Bending down he replaced his hand with his mouth, kissing her, nibbling her skin as he went, up, down then back up again. Then he strayed. Right where she wanted him. To her breasts. He circled each nipple with his tongue before he drew her left nipple into his mouth for a sensual suck.

Before she lost her mind due to pleasure, Tabby reached between and unbuttoned his shirt. Shaky fingers or not she needed to start getting him undressed.

"You taste so sweet. Better than any dessert I've ever made." He sucked again and she moaned. Loudly. "Oh, you like that too, don't you? I want to be the only man to ever taste you again."

Finally Tabby pulled the last button from the hole. Her hands enjoyed his bare chest, his abs, the strong muscles that tensed and flexed in his back. A light sheen of perspiration coated his skin but she didn't care. He was hot for her. And she was just as hot for him. A scream almost escaped her lips as Nico bit her nipple lightly before abandoning them for her lips. She loved kissing. Loved kissing him. Loved his taste, the way his tongue invaded her mouth so sweetly, the way he teased her with his teeth before he sucked her lip into his mouth.

When he leaned against her the hair on his chest tickled her nipples sending a double dose of sensation to her body. His mouth tickled hers while his chest did the same. But Nico wasn't done yet. His hand skimmed down her body and landed at the juncture between her thighs. She gasped in preparation for what would come next.

Nico push two fingers inside her. "So soft, so wet." Her muscles hugged his fingers. God he couldn't wait to bury his cock inside her. Her silky heat closed around his fingers while he started to pump them inside her. He couldn't get enough of her. All thoughts of their talk fled his mind. All he felt, all his thoughts circled around the woman writhing beneath him. Her pleasure, her happiness, her heart he wanted it all and right then he knew he would have it. No matter what he'd show her he was everything she'd been waiting for.

"You're body is so responsive to me, Tabby. You feel so good and I'm not even inside you yet." Nico returned to her breasts, licking her pert nipples and sucking them deeply into his mouth. He could feel her body start to tighten while her channel became more slick. She was so close. She panted beneath him, each breath becoming faster, more shallow.

He wasn't letting her go. Not know. This intense, primal feeling surged inside him crushing any doubts of their future together. He wanted her completely with no doubts from her. He wouldn't push. That wasn't his style. But would find out what held her back and he would show her how he felt. And the first order of business to get inside her. To show her how perfectly they fit together. First, he'd give her an orgasm, a prequel to what he had in store for her.

With his thumb, Nico began to circle her swollen clitoris. Her body lurched beneath him. Not slowing his movements in any way he bent toward her ear. "You like that don't you, *Tesoro?* I like it too. No, I fucking love it. Love to feel your silky body."

"Yes, I love it too."

He heard her struggle to get the words out, her speech breathless and sexy as hell. "I can feel your body tightening. You're ready to come." He increased the pressure to her clitoris. Swirling his thumb around her nub while his tongue dipped into her ear. That's all it took. Tabby let loose, her nails in his back and panting his name.

He'd never grow tired of this. Of her. If he'd have known love felt like this he would have claimed her a long time ago.

Drained from her climax Tabby lie still beneath Nico. His jeans felt rough against her legs. The silk of the shirt hanging from his shoulder felt cool against her over-sensitive skin. She could hardly move. The eagerness her body felt for him helped the muscles in her body react. With a hand against his chest Tabby pushed Nico off her. He helped her along by rolling onto the bed next to her.

Leaning up Nico pulled his shirt off before he went for the button on his pants. His sharp movements told her he felt the fervent need that exploded inside her own body. While he worked his pants down his legs Tabby reached in her bedside table and grabbed a condom package. She ripped open the foil just as he threw his pants to the floor. A second later she had the condom rolled down his pulsing, hot erection. In the blink of an eye Nico had her flipped onto her back beneath him.

But he didn't enter her. He lay above her staring into her eyes.

"Come on. What's taking so long?" she laughed but the situation was anything but funny. She wanted, no needed him. Now.

"Is my little wanton eager for me?"

"You know I am."

"Do you have any idea how much I want you, Tabby? What being inside you feels like?"

"No." Her reply wasn't completely true. If it felt anything like it did to her then she had an idea. No one filled her with the overwhelming need that Nico did. She'd never craved someone, body and soul like she did this man.

"Let me tell you." He pushed forward entering her slowly, inch my inch. "Your body hugs me like you were made for me, Tabby. So tight, so perfect around my cock."

He pushed farther inside. She almost came right there. He stretched her in the most delicious way.

"God you're hot, inside and out. Your heat surrounds me. Hot, wet, tight. Damn I could do this everyday for the rest of my life, baby. Be buried inside you. All the time."

Finally he buried himself to the hilt. He pushed his body tightly against her. She felt him everywhere. The hair on his legs scratching hers, his chest covering her, his hips, his crotch right where she needed him. "Move Nico. I want to make love to you."

The second the words left her mouth she regretted them. But right now she couldn't let herself care. Making love is exactly what this was to her and in the heat of the moment she could do nothing but admit it. Later, she'd think about it later. Right now nothing filled her mind but Nico and the way he started to pump so perfectly inside of her.

Tabby matched him, thrust for thrust enjoying the passion that overtook her. She heard Nico whispering to her but in her blissful daze she couldn't make out his words. When had mumbles ever sounded so sexy? Everything he did dripped of masculine sensuality like no man she'd ever known. Wanting to feel his hard body as he filled her, Tabby gripped his tight rear end. Soon she felt herself pushing him against her, she needed all of him as deep as possible.

Firecrackers of delight started to pop inside her preparing her body for what would come next. The pleasure built, stronger and stronger, her orgasm gaining strength with each of Nico's movements. She felt him nip her neck, kiss her behind the ear and it was all too much. An atomic bomb exploded her into the most powerful release she'd ever had. Nico kept going, once, twice, three more powerful thrusts before his body collapsed on top of hers.

"Damn. I'm so going to pass out." Tabby closed her eyes. Nico rolled her to her side so she faced him. Her eyes flickered open only to get lost in the dark depths of his.

"What happened this week, Tabby?"

His voice sounded smooth, comforting. She knew this was coming. Thought maybe she could put it off with the lure of sleep but Nico's voice told his determination. He wouldn't let her sidetrack him again. When she opened her mouth to respond, shock hit her at what she said. "My parents were the most loving people. They had such a wonderful relationship. Did I ever tell you that?"

As if he knew she needed comfort Nico brought his hand to the side of her head, his thumb making circles on her face while his fingers played with her hair. "No you haven't. I'd like to hear now."

Unable to speak, Tabby lay next to him, fingering the hairs on his chest, thinking about the words that wanted to come but couldn't.

"You can tell me anything, *Tesoro*. Trust me."

"I'm lucky really. My life has been so much easier than most. I had the nice upper-middle class upbringing, two parents in the home. I never wanted for anything. Hell, we even had a damn housekeeper." She reveled in the sensation of Nico's fingers stroking her. In his arms she felt so comfortable, so cared for. The thing is she didn't know if it was real or a façade. Didn't know if the concern pooling in his dark eyes meant what she hoped it did.

"God my parents were in love. You could see it in everything they did. The looks they shared, the Friday night dates. He brought her flowers for no reason, never forgot an anniversary, he would do anything for her. They ran their home and their company together. They were strict and harsh in the business world but completely loving with each other."

Nico opened his mouth, his voice, low, serious. "But what about you, *Tesoro?* I don't hear anything about you in all this."

"That's because I didn't fit into their lives." That hurt to say. Two people who had so much love to give and they couldn't give any to her. How could that be? Was she so unlovable?

"They never hugged me, never kissed me, I could never climb in bed with them if I had a bad dream. It's like they didn't have enough left for me. They pampered each other but they didn't care enough to share any of that love with me." She could feel the tears coming. A sting hit her eyes and they began to pool with moisture.

"I had no siblings, my grandparents weren't around. I had no one until I met Bri and Kaylee. All I've ever wanted is to be loved. Is that too much to ask?" He shoulders started to shake as she let her walls come down and cried. She couldn't hold it back anymore. She didn't want to. Not with Nico. He gave her a comfort she'd never had before. Quietly he held her and let her cry.

His hand ran through her hair, his lips tickled her face. Who knows how long she let the tears flow. But she needed to get this out and it felt right letting Nico in on this part of her life. He'd touched her deeply. More than expected. More than any the other men she'd dated in the past who she thought seemed so right from the get go. This sensitive, caring man that she found in Nico was unexpected. But damn she loved it. Loved him.

Closing her eyes, Tabby soaked in the feel of the pad of his finger as it wiped the tears from her face. He kissed each eyelid.

"Look at me."

She did.

"Thank God you found yourself an Italian man." His hand moved to rub her bare shoulder making bumps of pleasure pebble on her skin. "You want amore? Big family? Hell my Mama and my sisters have never met a stranger. We'll love you, take care of you, feed you. Mama will want to know everything about you, give you advice when you don't need, but it's all out of love."

He leaned in and kissed her.

"And don't forget the kisses. I hope you like kissing, Tesoro. Kisses hello, kisses goodbye. We're very affectionate people, you know."

She couldn't help but let out a small laugh. Some of the heaviness in her chest lifted. He always made her feel good, always knew what to say to make her smile. He smiled too, a bone melting smile that turned her into a pile of mush. She'd always dreamed about a man who could turn her into mush with just one look. Sounded funny but it was true. Little did she know she'd find it in the most unexpected place.

A second later his smile disappeared. His face turning serious. "All playfulness aside, baby, now look at me." When she tried to divert her eyes Nico touched the underside of her chin with his finger and tilted her head up. "This is important and I want to make sure you're paying attention. You deserve a whole hell of a lot more than the shitty way your parents

Unexpected Mr. Right   **167**

treated you as a child."

"I doubt they hurt me on purpose. I just wasn't enough. Didn't fit into the little world they locked themselves away in."

"That's bullshit, Tabby."

"Then why didn't they love me?"

An angry tick worked in his jaw. She'd never seen this angry side of him before.

"Whatever they shared wasn't love. If they had love to give each other they should have had enough for their daughter. I don't know what really went on behind closed doors with your parents but I'll never believe they were this happy, loving couple. Not after the way they treated you. You deserve so much more, baby. You deserve everything."

"Then why couldn't the two people who were supposed to love me unconditionally find a place in their heart for me?"

"I don't know. I wish I could tell you. But I do know one thing, they didn't deserve you. You have such a big, beautiful heart and you will get all those things you want; the husband, the kids." Nico rolled her to her back and made himself comfortable between her legs. "You're going to make a great wife someday, Tabby. The best mom. God your kids will love you. I know it."

She smiled internally. Her heart felt lighter, like it could float on air. The conviction he spoke with gave her a hope she hadn't felt in a long time, if ever. He renewed her confidence. She had friends who loved her and would do anything for her and a boyfriend who might not love her but he did care about her. She saw it in all the things he did for her, the way he spoke to her. She just feared in the end she wouldn't be enough for him either.

No matter what she wanted him to know how she felt. Whether or not he'd want to hear it she owed it to herself to speak the words. If in the end they walked away from each other she'd know she was woman enough to utter those three magical words to him. "So all this time I should have just been looking for an Italian man? Damn, if I'd have known." She teased him, showing him the playful part of herself that he helped her find. The part that would help her through rough times.

"No I think you misunderstood me." His voice was slow, sensual, serious. The three s's all in once sentence.

"But you just said-" He silenced her by nibbling on her bottom lip. Who'd have known a nibble could be so damn sexy? He kissed just her bottom lip, sucked it in his mouth then pulled away.

"Not any Italian man. This man."

"Wait," Tabby told him before he could say anymore. She didn't know if this conversation would go where it sounded like it might and she needed to get this out first. "I want to tell you something but before I do I want you're word you won't respond. Good or bad, I don't want to hear it tonight."

He watched her, concern darkening his eyes. She needed him to agree to this before she went any further. After he heard what she had to say she didn't want him reply out of obligation either because of her feelings or because of her past.

"You have my word, *Tesoro*."

Tabby ignored the loud echo in her head as blood rushed through her body. She wouldn't let nerves distract her. Not tonight. "I know you're not looking for vows. I know that you have no plans for the white picket fence and two point five kids but I need you to know something." She inhaled and exhaled a deep breath. "I love you. More than anything. All my life I thought I knew what I wanted in a man but I was wrong. It's you my heart has been waiting for."

The darkness in his eyes disappeared as he widened them, staring down at her. His eyebrows rose, most likely automatically. His lips twitched, whether out of fear or excitement she didn't know. Then he smiled before saying, "I—"

Tabby put her hand to his mouth. "No you promised. Just kiss me Nico. I need to feel you make love to me again."

His lips lowered to hers as he granted her request. They made love slowly, passionately, touching, caressing, whispering. He buried himself as deeply as possible inside her until they both came together. They knew each other's bodies so well in such a short amount of time. When he pulled out of her, Nico pulled her against him, holding her in a tight, comforting grip.

"Oh, and did I mention earlier that Italian men are also really good in the sack?" he asked.

Tabby laughed snuggling as close to him as possible. *Only Nico,* she thought. "So does this one go for all Italian men?"

"Nope. Just like before, only this one."

The hand he had around her started to tickle her naked arm. She felt her eyes begin to droop and didn't try to stop them. Her body relaxed exhausted from their lovemaking. A few minutes later in the back of her mind she heard Nico's confident, masculine voice call her name. She didn't have the energy to respond.

In a softer almost faint voice she heard four words fill her heart with hope.

"I love you too."

She was too afraid to open her eyes incase it was a dream.

Chapter Thirteen

The next couple of days passed in a whirlwind of wedding preparations. Everything needed to be finalized this week. And since she was "the wedding chick" as Bri called her she offered to help do most of it. She hadn't been at work all week but she'd still hardly had a second to sit down, much less see Nico. Finally she had a couple spare minutes. A couple hours earlier she'd done a sample of the flower arrangement that she would do this weekend for the wedding. She'd done a mock boutonnière too.

Spur of the moment she decided to run by Luciano's and see if Nico was there. She missed him. He still didn't know she'd heard him tell her he loved her a few nights before. Her heart tickled at the thought of hearing those words from his mouth. She just hoped they were sincere. Not that she thought Nico would purposefully mislead her. He wouldn't. That she knew but still, could a man who never wanted to settle down really fall in love as quickly as they had?

But then she'd fallen love with him quickly too and even though she'd been the opposite of him and longed to settle down she knew that had nothing to do with her feelings for him. Her love for him grew because of the man himself. He was more caring and generous than she'd given him credit for. Without trying he'd shown her what it felt like to really mean something to someone, to have someone who did things just to

Unexpected Mr. Right
171

see her smile, not because it benefited them. Like their trip to Half Moon bay. He'd put thought into making their weekend special to make her smile and that meant more than he could ever know.

But did that mean love? She didn't know. He'd loved his single life and she feared the monotony of having a real, lasting relationship might bore him.

Tabby opened the door to Luciano's and walked inside. Luciano stood with the hostess looking over a piece of paper. He looked up when she approached him.

"Hey Tabby. How are you?"

"I'm good. I just stopped by to see Nico for a second. If he's busy I can come back."

Luciano shook his head. "Are you kidding me? He'd have my ass if I sent you away. I actually think he's in my office. Go ahead and go back there."

She smiled as she walked past him. "Thanks Luciano."

"Not a problem." He turned to continue his conversation with his hostess.

Tabby headed toward Luciano's office excitement racing through her body. Damn she was really in trouble. She loved this man so much. She couldn't wait to see him again. As she approached Luciano's office she heard voices drifting through the door that stood cracked open. The excitement died as dread filled her belly making her nauseous. She heard Nico inside and to her surprise Cindy, the woman who'd interrupted their very first kiss, the one who got her the name Slugger.

Tabby couldn't help herself. Quietly she leaned next to the door and listened. She knew it was wrong but her fear surpassed her conscience at the moment.

"You're looking good, Nico."

He hesitated a moment before he replied. "Thanks Cindy. You look good too."

"I've missed you. We had some good times together."

"Yes we did."

"It's been a long time, Nico. Too long."

"Listen, Cindy—"

"I don't want to listen. I want to taste you instead."

Then she heard nothing. Anger, confusion, pain all exploded in her body making her knees weak. They had to be kissing. She knew it. Why would he do that? Why would he hurt her like this? God, how could she have been so stupid? A zebra couldn't change their strips. He may have said he wanted a relationship with her but she should have known it wouldn't last long. She should have known she wouldn't be enough for him. Tabby felt tears begin to sting her eyes. Before she could make a fool of herself she turned and walked away.

Nico knew he needed to tread lightly. Cindy had a glint in her eyes that told him she'd come here for one thing and one thing only. Sex. If he'd had any doubts in the past, which he didn't, he knew right now that Tabby was the only woman for him. The thought of touching another woman, of having another woman touch him, nauseated him. Her come-hither eyes made him want to do nothing but turn and run the other way.

He wanted his woman and no one else would do. But still, they had a past that included filling each other's needs whenever the mood struck them. It was very obvious that Cindy was in the mood right now. He had to approach this very cautiously. She reached for him. Nico stepped away. "Cindy we need to talk."

"Talking is overrated. I'd much rather set up a time and place for us to meet tonight. We could kiss on it."

He held up his hand to stop her from getting any closer. "I've met someone else."

"So? We don't have any commitments to each other, Nico. That's part of why we've worked in the past."

This was going to be harder than he thought. "You don't understand. I fell in love with someone, Cindy."

"What's love got to do with it, baby?"

Unexpected Mr. Right   **173**

Damn. What had he ever seen in her? *A nice surgically enhanced rack and the fact that she's into the whole no strings attached thing.* It sickened him. The things that had previously attracted him the most now disgusted him. How could he have been so shallow? No wonder it had taken Tabby so long to even give him the time of day. "Everything. Things are different for me now, Cindy. There's only one woman for me."

She looked shocked. "You're serious? Mr. Fun-loving, San Francisco's biggest flirt has decided to settle into the one woman, one man till death do us part kind of life? Come on Nico. You'll be bored in a month."

How wrong she was. Tabby excited him in ways no one ever had. "That's where you're wrong. I'm not going to defend my relationship to you but know I could never be bored with Tabitha. She's everything to me."

"Wow, lucky lady." Her demeanor changed in a flash. She kissed his cheek. "Tell Tabitha she's one lucky lady. And if you ever come to your senses you know where to find me." She winked at him and left the office.

Luciano walked in right behind her. "I didn't know she was here. What did Tabby say when she saw her here with you?"

"What do you mean? I haven't seen Tabby all day."

"I sent her back here a little while ago. You didn't see her?"

Shit, shit, shit. He had a really bad feeling right now. "How long ago?"

"Just a few minutes."

"Fuck." Nico ran a hand through his already messy hair and stalked the room. "I wonder why she didn't say anything to me."

Luciano sat in the chair behind his desk. "Sorry, Nic. If I'd have known Cindy was back here I wouldn't have sent Tabby."

"I have nothing to hide. I don't care that she came back here I just want to know why she didn't say anything to me."

"Maybe she got the wrong idea somehow."

"I'm going to call her." Nico walked out of the office and pulled his black cell phone from his pocket and dialed Tabby's phone number. It went straight to her voice mail. She had her phone off and for some reason he didn't think it was a coincidence. She could be stubborn as hell when she got an idea in her head. And he knew without question she'd overheard some of his conversation with Cindy and jumped to conclusions. The more he thought about it the more it pissed him off.

He'd never given her a reason to doubt him yet she did at every turn of the road. He knew her past had something to do with it but if they were to ever have any kind of real relationship she had to have a little bit of faith in him. He hated that she doubted him so much. No matter what he did, how much fun they had together she didn't seem to know him at all.

She claimed to love him yet she thought him the kind of man that would sneak around behind her back? The part that angered him the most is that she didn't even talk to him, didn't respect him enough to tell him what she'd heard, or what she thought she heard. And he's the one who was new at relationships?

He knew enough to know that relationships took trust and no matter how much he showed her he cared she didn't believe him. Her actions today showed him that. Nico couldn't live like that. He loved her but he needed her to trust him. He needed her not to doubt him. Part of him thanked God she hadn't heard him tell her he loved her. Not that she would have believed him anyway but if or when he told her he wanted to be sure they were on the same page. That they both knew what it took to make a relationship work and they believed in each other. Not just him believing in her.

As hard as it would be, he wasn't going to call her. He couldn't. If this relationship had any hope of lasting she had to give him a little bit of faith.

Tabby set a brown paper grocery bag on her kitchen counter and unloaded their "girl's night in" necessities. Instead of

Unexpected Mr. Right   175

going to Luciano's tonight, she, Bri and Tabby planned a
sleepover at her house. Yeah, kind of silly but they didn't care.
Tonight would be Kaylee's last Friday night as a single woman
and they wanted to celebrate no men allowed. Not that any of
them had men to worry about except the bride herself. Bri
didn't have a man and Tabby lost hers.

Nico hadn't so much as called her and the sad part is he
didn't even know she'd caught him with Cindy the serpent.
Obviously when propositioned by another woman he quickly
forgot he'd been the one to suggest they have a relationship.
And he'd also been the one to return her vow of love if only
when he didn't think she heard him. Tabby pulled out a bottle
of rum, strawberries, and daiquiri mix. Usually she'd drink
wine but tonight called for the big guns. She had a sexy Italian
to drink out of her mind.

Yeah, like that will work. She left the alcohol on the counter
and put the rest of the food away before trashing the bag. She
really did look forward to tonight. Nothing helped get her
head on straight like spending time with the girls. Tonight
they'd talk, laugh, and probably cry celebrating Kaylee's
goodbye to bachelorettehood. Who cares that that
bachelorettehood wasn't even a real word. That's exactly what
they were doing. She only hoped along the way Nico would
slip out of her head. Because so far he hadn't left since she
heard him in Luciano's office on Wednesday.

She didn't understand the whole situation. They'd gotten to
know each other. She thought she knew him well. Never
would she have expected him to do something like this. Sure
she wondered if he'd get tired of dating her, if he'd realize a
relationship isn't what he really wanted but she'd never
thought him the type to sneak around behind her back. She
never thought he'd drop her and never even pick up the phone
to tell her.

Her fears already crept back into her heart. She had a feeling
they'd now be taking up permanent residency there. No one
would give her that unconditional, forever kind of love that
her heart longed for. Had she really expected anything

different? The sad truth is she did. Nico started making her hope that the man she loved more than anyone else would feel the same about her.

Before she started to cry and ruined her best friends party before it had the chance to start, Tabby, pushed a button on her stereo, Beyonce filled the air as she headed to her bedroom to change. She needed to stop thinking of Nico. She had a bachelorette party to get ready for and this weekend a wedding to help run. And it would be perfect. If she couldn't have her dreams at least Kaylee could.

Tabby hit the puree button on her blender, one drink already in her system. As the loud spin of blades filled the air chunks of ice, strawberry and rum began to fly as well. A chunk flew at Bri hitting her in the face as she reached to grab a bowl from the cabinet next to her. Oops. She felt a slight buzz already. She could have sworn she'd put that lid on the blender.

"Girl, thank God you never tried to be a bartender," Bri wiped off her cheek and picked up the lid. "See this? It's called a lid. You put it on top of the blender." She gave her friend a laugh and a wink.

Bri went back to standing on her tiptoes and trying to get into the cabinet. Tabby grabbed an ice cube from the tray and stuck it down her friend's shirt. "Oops. Damn I'm clumsy tonight."

Brianna started to do a bouncing dance in the middle of her kitchen reaching for the ice cube that must have somehow gotten stuck in her bra. When she pulled it out she started chasing Tabby around the kitchen threatening to retaliate, cube in hand. When Tabby rounded the kitchen she slipped in some daiquiri mix that made it to the floor and went down, Bri was right behind her. And that's when the laughing fit began.

They rolled on the floor, Bri still trying to get Tabby back with the ice cube. A second later, Kaylee came in.

"Damn, I always miss the fun."

Unexpected Mr. Right

"Help me up." Tabby tried to fight Bri off while reaching up to Kaylee. Gullible she reached down to help and Tabby pulled her down with them. When she did, Kaylee's hand caught on the blender knocking it over and spilling the rest of the strawberry daiquiri mix on top of them. They all sat there quiet for a minute, Tabby on the bottom, Bri had a hold on her shoulders and Kaylee had fallen onto her lap. Daiquiri mix dripped from Tabby's head, down Bri's arm and over Kaylee's back.

Tabby shook her head and the excess liquid flew in droplets at her friends. The flood gates opened bringing a wave of loud, joyful laughter. God if anyone walked in right now they'd think them crazy, a sticky strawberry pile of women laughing on the kitchen floor. A few minutes later, when her cheeks started to hurt Tabby finally slowed her laughing. She loved these girls. A few hours ago she'd never imagined laughing like she was right now. They were the only one's who could make her laugh like this despite the way she felt.

"Um, I'm not even going to ask how this happened." Kaylee stood up. Both Brianna and Tabby were right behind her.

"Get three women, and empty house, an upcoming wedding and alcohol together and things are bound to get a little bit crazy." Brianna added.

"Yeah I hope your future husband knows what he's in for. I say next month we take this to your house." Tabby teased Kaylee.

"I think the wrestling on the kitchen floor would have turned out a little bit different if men were here." Kaylee said.

"I'd like to get my wrestle on with one man in particular." Bri made a fist with one hand and punched her other bouncing on her toes like a boxer.

"Whatever you say, Brianna. I think you want Jackson more than you want to admit. I have a feeling if the two of you got together it would be the same kind of wrestling I like with Luciano or the kind Tabby and Nico have been doing lately." Kaylee laughed. Tabby socked her in the arm.

"Puleeze girl. I wouldn't want Monty if he was the last man

on earth."

"Monty?" Both Kaylee and Tabby said in unison.

"His last name is Montgomery. I call him Monty just to piss his Majesty off."

"You're so bad, Bri. We'll let the whole Jackson thing go for now because we have bigger fish to fry with Tabby. I need the 411 on what's been up with you and Nico lately. You haven't been quite so moony eyed lately."

Tabby turned for her kitchen door. "There's nothing to know. I'll be right back. I need to get changed."

A few minutes later they were cleaned up, changed into their night clothes, had a new daiquiri in hand, and sat cross legged on Tabby's living room carpet. Tabby took a drink, the cold briefly shocking her mouth before she set her glass down on a coaster on her coffee table. Neither Bri or Kaylee had said much since they finished changing.

"Let's play sleepover games like we used to when we were younger." Kaylee suggested.

Surprised, Tabby turned to Kaylee and said, "You want to play sleepover games at your bachelorette party?"

"Sure. I'm *having* a sleepover so why can't we play the games. You know, kind of as a goodbye to adolescence and hello to Holy matrimony." Her eyes held a curious glint that made Tabby wonder what she was up to.

"You're the one taking the plunge from a cliff. I guess you should get to pick your last meal." Bri smacked her own hand. "Oops. Did I say that? I never know when to keep my mouth shut."

They all giggled before agreeing to Kaylee's wish. "So what are we going to play?" Tabby asked.

"Truth or Dare."

Oh boy. What did Kaylee have up her pajama sleeve?

"And since I'm the woman of the hour I get to go first." Kaylee turned toward Tabby. "Truth or Dare?"

Unexpected Mr. Right   **179**

Oh shit. She should have known this had more to do with her than Kaylee's sudden urge to pretend to be a giddy sixteen year old girl. "I don't want to get into this tonight, Kaylee. It's your night."

"I have no idea what you're talking about. Truth or dare?" Kaylee asked again.

"Fine. Dare." At least she wouldn't have to answer questions this way.

"I dare you to call Nico." Bri high-fived Kaylee at her request.

"Agh. I'm going to get you guys back for this. I change to truth." The words grudgingly fell from her mouth.

"Did something bad go down with you and Nico recently?"

"Yes," Tabby replied simply.

"What?" they both asked.

"Nope that was your question. My turn. Brianna truth or dare?"

"I'm not the one who picked on you. You should have chosen Ms. Ball and Chain over there." When both girls gave her the don't go there look Bri, said, "Fine. I'll go with truth to."

Two could play at this game. "Do you find Jackson attractive?"

A look of dread came over Bri's face but she quickly hid it by shrugging her shoulder nonchalantly. "Yeah. Who wouldn't. The man is fine with a capital F. That doesn't mean he's not an asshole who I wish would fall off the face of the earth though."

"Yeah sure," Kaylee added.

"Whatever." Brianna turned toward Tabby. "You know the drill, Tab, truth or dare."

"What about Kaylee?"

"I can take a turn if it makes you feel better."

"It does." Tabby took another drink before crossing her arms.

"Come on, Tab. We all know this game is really about you. Might as well just tell us what we want to know."

"You sound like a B rated cop flick. What are you two good cop bad cop? Or bad cop and badder I should say since this was Kaylee's idea anyway." Both girls just looked at her waiting for Tabby to give in and tell them what happened. "Fine I'll tell you. I went and fell in love with him. Stupid I know."

"No one said that, Tabby." Kaylee looked at her with sensitive eyes.

"I know but I'm sure you're thinking it. I know I am. It's just," Tabby let a rush of air leave her lungs before continuing. "We were spending all that time together and he showed me how sweet he can really be. He's so different than any man I've ever known. I thought I got to know the real him. I thought our friendship led to something. He makes me feel special, makes me laugh, and there's such a physical connection between us. I've never felt anything like it."

"So what's the prob?" Bri asked.

"I walked in on him with Cindy."

For some reason, Kaylee didn't sound convinced when she asked, "Walked in on them doing something they shouldn't or you just assumed they were?"

"Well I didn't actually see anything. I overheard them and left before I had the chance to see him with the skank."

"Oh, harsh, Tabby. What did he do to make you think he'd cheat on you? I can't really see Nico doing that."

A tidal wave of guilt washed over her. Just as quickly it drifted back out to sea. He'd always told her he never planned to settle down. From the get go she knew they were only biding time. He'd get bored and move on quickly. She didn't need to see it with her own eyes to know what happened after she left. Just like with everyone else she wasn't enough for him. She knew that. The time had come to move on. "He's always been a ladies man and you guys know it. I got myself in over my head. I think somehow I hoped I could change him but I couldn't."

"So you're giving up? You decided you didn't really love him?" Kaylee asked.

Tabby couldn't believe what her friend said. Shock made her words stumble from her mouth. "Of course I really love him. He's the complete opposite of what I always thought I wanted but my heart tells me he's everything I need. He's fun, playful but can also be serious. He has a kind heart, tries to make me happy and the fact is just being around him makes me happy. He's everything to me."

And that's when it hit her. Not just a little love tap either. A knock-out punch to the heart and mind with the strength of a Mike Tyson punch. Even though in the beginning Nico wasn't what she thought she wanted he was exactly what she *needed*. He gave her that unconditional love that she wanted. Who knows if he knew it or not but he did. She claimed to love him but she ran at the first little setback. She cowered and believed the worst in him without giving him the benefit of the doubt.

How could she expect him to fall in love with her, to give a real relationship a try if she didn't love him enough to fight for him, to believe in the man she knew him to be? He told her he loved her when he had nothing to prove, nothing to get out of it and she'd thrown that away because of half a conversation through an office door. His small day to day actions told her his true character and she'd denied that because she was scared.

She made herself doubt him, when that's the one thing he'd asked her not to do so that she could walk away before he had the chance to hurt her. He'd given her clues all along. Even before his whispered words of love in bed a few nights before. He'd asked for a relationship with her, he'd spent all his time with her, he'd made her see how much she deserved to be loved. And she'd thrown it away. Inside she knew she looked for a reason to run but not anymore. She loved this man and she would fight for him. "Kay, ask me again."

"Um, I'm a little lost here. Ask you what?"

"Truth or dare."

She looked a little confused but Kaylee asked her anyway, "Truth or dare?"

"Dare."

As if a light clicked on in her head Kaylee told her. "I dare you to go and talk to Nico."

Tabby jumped to her feet the blood pumping vigorously through her veins. She turned to Bri, "Call me a cab." Then she hugged Kaylee, "Sorry I ruined your night but I have to do this. You know I love—"

Kaylee pulled away, "Shut up and go get dressed. You have a man to win back." Kaylee's smile told her she didn't give a damn about the ruined bachelorette party. She wanted her friend to be happy and for the first time in a long time Tabby knew her dream floated within her grasp.

The cab pulled up in front of Nico's apartment at 11:32 PM. They'd made a pit stop at an ice cream joint and made it to Nico's in record time. Tabby tossed a wad of cash at him, not caring how much she overpaid him before jumping out of the car and closing the door with a slam. She raced to his door, her flip-flops flapping as she ran. She hadn't cared what she put on to come over here. Her hair was a mess. She had on a loose fitting pair of sweat pants, a black bra with a white tank. She knew she broke all kinds of fashion laws but right now that didn't matter. With a heavy fist she banged on his door impatiently.

A couple seconds later she did it again. When he opened the door she pushed her way inside and closed it. He'd been asleep. His jaw had a light dusting of stubble, his hair ruffled in a delicious mess of raven black locks on his head, and he wore a pair of gray boxer briefs and nothing else. If she didn't have something important to tell him she would have jumped him right then and there. "I'm not giving up on you. In my heart I know you didn't do anything with Cindy and if you did, then that woman is going to have a fight on her hands because you're mine and I'm not willing to let you go."

There. What do you have to say about that?

"Tabby I—"

Unexpected Mr. Right
183

She cut him off before he could finish. "I love you Nico and I know you love me to. I heard you tell me the other night and even if I hadn't I can see it in your eyes. In the way you treat me. Maybe I've been blind until tonight but I'm telling you right now I can see."

A minute passed before a half smile tugged at his mouth.

"You're right, *Tesoro*. I do love you. But I don't know if we can fix this. You have no faith in me. From day one I've had to trick, beg and plead you in some way or another just to spend time with you. I've tried to be everything you want and the fact is no matter how much I try I don't know if you'll ever be satisfied with me. The first chance you had you ran from me. You assumed the worst and didn't trust me enough to give me the benefit of the doubt.

"I've done everything I can to make you see how much you mean to me. I broke all my own rules, asked if we could make our relationship official, introduced you to my family, fell in love but it wasn't enough for you to believe in me. I'm just not that knight in shining armor type that you want and I'm not willing to be anything different than who I am. Just like I'd never expect you to be anything different than who you are." He leaned against a table by his front door.

His words hurt but she knew they were true. At least the parts about her were. She hadn't believed in him like she should, never gave him the benefit of the doubt, didn't see him as more than the ladies man she'd always thought him to be even when he showed her he was so much more. "You're right. I had so many things I wanted that I failed to give you what you deserved. I put blinders up because I thought you weren't who I thought I wanted and that is wrong. And the fact is you aren't what I wanted, Nico, you're so much more.

"You know how to love better than any man I've ever known. You know how to make everyone you love feel like the most important person on the world. You'd never shaft your children because you have enough love for everyone. You're honest, loyal, and passionate in love and life. I have fun with you, can share anything with you, and even though I don't deserve it I'm asking you to give me another chance because you're *it* for me.

"Even though I dreamed about love, preached about it to my friends, and wished for it in reality I never thought it would happen for me. Never thought I'd find that one person who could be everything, who would love me for me and when I did I didn't love you for you. I didn't expect to find love, Nico. I pushed the only true shot I had away and I'm sorry about that. But I'm telling you now I couldn't find anyone more right for me than you are. I can promise you I'll never doubt you again."

Her heart ached, the muscle thumped, felt like it might explode in her chest. She'd done wrong by him. She knew that. If he didn't forgive her it would be her own fault but God she hoped he did. She wanted to laugh with him, cook with him, grow old with him, love him. But the longer he sat there with an empty stare, the black depths of his eyes boring a hole in her heart she began to realize that she might not get to do any of those things. She may have lost him forever.

Never in a million years did Nico expect her to lay out her heart for him the way she just did. Her voice spoke with sincerity that even if he wanted to doubt he couldn't. And he didn't want to doubt it. No matter how pissed he'd been at her he had to forgive her. She was his and holding out these past couple days had been hell on him. He wanted her forever, to stake claim on her, to wipe all doubt out of her mind as to who he wanted in his bed and his heart for the rest of his life.

Seeing her tonight confirmed his feelings for her. She'd put her heart out there, entrusted it to him and he'd be damned before he bruised it much less let it break. She looked so sweet, so rumpled, so damned sexy that he couldn't hold himself back anymore. Nico took three long strides forward to stand in front of her. Hungry to touch her he reached out and took her face in his hands before he lowered his mouth to kiss her. More like devour her.

Tabby gave just as deeply as she took as their tongues mated in a kiss that rocked his world. Oh yeah. This was his woman, his treasure and he planned to keep her. He pulled away from her delicious mouth to say, "It took you long enough, *Tesoro*."

Pure happiness exploded in her eyes. Damn he loved seeing that look on her face. Loved even more that he is the man who put it there.

"You know you can trust me, baby. I love you." He realized that he'd only spoken those words to her one other time besides tonight. Even then she'd been asleep. Because they felt so good he opened his mouth to say them again, "I love you, Tabby. I could get used to saying that." He wrapped his arms around her, pulling her close as he peered down at her.

"I can get used to hearing them. I love you too, Nico."

"What's that?" he asked tilting his head toward the bag.

"Ice cream. I wanted you to know I can be rocky road but only for you, Nico."

"Damn baby. I've known all along you were rocky road." He kissed her. "But you're right. Only for me."

"I love you so much, Nico."

"You just love me because I can cook for you." Man he enjoyed giving her a hard time. "But you know we're going to have to get a little more serious about those cooking lessons. A man needs a day off every now and again."

She playfully pushed him away. "You just want me barefoot, pregnant and in the kitchen." Her eyes widened like she regretted what she said. "I didn't really mean that. Not pushing you into the whole baby and marriage thing."

He bent down dropping a swift kiss to her lips. "No? That's the second time you've mentioned barefoot and pregnant to me."

"I was joking. I'm really not pushing anything on you, Nico."

"Guess I'm going to have to be the one pushing you then."

Epilogue

Tabby rocked to the slow beat of the music while Nico held her tightly in his arms. People danced all around them but to her, they were the only two people in the room. His hand slowly caressed the open back of her pale yellow maid of honor dress as if savoring the feel of her. His hard body molded against her like they were meant to be like this, in each others arms, becoming as close as two people could be.

"Remind me again why we have to stay for the whole reception." His voice whispered low into her ear. "I want to ravage you."

Tabby let out a slight giggle. "Because you're the best man and I'm a maid of honor?"

"Damn. See what we get for all the hard work we put into this wedding? They're holding us hostage so I can't take you home and rip that sexy yellow dress off you."

He bent and nuzzled her neck. Tabby reveled in the feel of his warmth against her neck before she replied. "I think that might have been his plan all along. Maybe the whole wedding is just a farce to keep you clothed and sexless."

"I think I've created a monster, *Tesoro*. Since when did you get such a good sense of humor?"

"Since you." She pulled away so she could look in his eyes. He meant everything to her. This is what love was. Not her parents, not any of the other relationships she'd had in the

Unexpected Mr. Right

past. This man standing in front of her embodied what the word love was all about.

"You keep that up and I'm going to get a big head."

Nico dipped his face down to hers and kissed her. A slow, passionate kiss that matched the beat of the music. Just as he pulled away the song ended. Kaylee and Luciano's day would soon be over but their lives were just starting. As was hers. The ceremony had gone off without a hitch. Kaylee made the perfect bride, and Tabby was blessed to walk down the aisle with the man she loved. It wasn't her own wedding but she didn't care. She had Nico and that's all that mattered.

About the Author:

Kelley Nyrae has loved writing for as long as she can remember. From the moment she won her first writing contest in the second grade she knew writing was her passion. Her plan had always been to write children's books but for one reason or another it never worked out. In 2005 she became a stay at home mom for the first time. That's when she picked up her first romance novel and fell in love. She knew that writing romance books is what she was meant to do and her life hasn't been the same ever since. All her dreams have come true!

Kelley has been blessed with a wonderful, supportive husband and two beautiful children who always bring a smile to her face. She resides in sunny Southern California.

Parker Publishing, LLC

Celebrating Black
Love Life Literature

Mail or fax orders to:
12523 Limonite Avenue Suite #440-438
Mira Loma, CA 91752
phone: (866) 205-7902 fax: (951) 685-8036 fax
or order from our Web site: www.parker-publishing.com
orders@parker-publishing.com

Ship to:

Name: _____

Address: _____

_____

City: _____

State: _____ Zip:_____

Phone: _____

Qty	Title	Price	Total

Shipping and handling is $3.50, Priority Mail shipping is $6.00 FREE standard shipping for orders over $30

Add S&H Alaska, Hawaii, and international orders – call for rates

CA residents add 7.75% sales tax

Payment methods: We accept Visa, MasterCard, Discovery, or money orders.
NO PERSONAL CHECKS.

Payment Method: (circle one): VISA MC DISC Money Order

Name on Card: _____

Card Number: _____ - ____

ExpDate: _____

Address: _____

_____

City: _____

State: _____ Zip:_____